# MAIL-ORDER BARONESS

## LORDS OF THE ROCKIES
### BOOK TWO

## MISTY M. BELLER

Misty M. Beller
BOOKS

Mail-Order Baroness

Copyright © 2025 Misty M. Beller

MistyMBeller.com

All rights reserved. No portion of this book may be reproduced or transmitted in any form or by any means—photocopied, shared electronically, scanned, stored in a retrieval system, or other—without the express permission of the publisher. Exceptions will be made for brief quotations used in critical reviews or articles promoting this work.

The characters and events in this fictional work are the product of the author's imagination. Any resemblance to actual people, living or dead, is coincidental.

Unless otherwise indicated, all Scripture quotations are taken from the Holy Bible, King James Version.

Scripture quotations taken from The Holy Bible, New International Version®, NIV®. Copyright © 1973, 1978, 1984, 2011 by Biblica, Inc. Used with permission of Zondervan. All rights reserved worldwide. www.zondervan.com

Cover design by Evelyne Labelle at Carpe Librum Book Design: www.carpelibrumbookdesign.com

ISBN-13 Trade Paperback: 978-1-965918-45-6

*He tends his flock like a shepherd:*
*He gathers the lambs in his arms*
*and carries them close to his heart;*
*he gently leads those that have young.*

*Isaiah 40:11 (NIV)*

# CHAPTER 1

Septe... 

September, 1869

Balfour Ranch, near Walnut Springs, Montana Territory

"What's going on?" James Balfour propped his elbows on the polished oak dining table, glancing around at his three brothers as his insides knotted. They'd all gathered at Enoch's request, which meant something serious. Especially since Enoch had sent the women outside for a walk to see the horses that were pastured nearest the house. In other words, out of earshot.

Enoch leaned forward, keeping his voice low. "We need help." The words hung in the air like smoke from Mrs. Wang's kitchen fire.

James arched a brow, scanning from one brother to the next. Enoch wasn't the sort to admit needing anything. "What kind of help?" Though he suspected the answer. He'd seen the fatigue in Mrs. Wang's face, the way she moved slower these days.

"For Mrs. Wang." Enoch's jaw worked. "She's kept this place running for years, never a word of complaint. But with

Mandie's condition..." He nodded toward the window, where his wife, very heavy with child, walked with their housekeeper. "And winter coming on early, it's too much for one person."

Enoch had a valid point. One James should have voiced already.

Thomas, youngest of them all, spoke up. "You're right. She's not getting any younger. The work's harder on her, even if she'd never say so."

The silence that followed felt final, as though they'd all known it and only now put it to words.

Robert nodded from across the table. "The preserving alone nearly did her in this year. All those vegetables from the garden, plus the meat from the cattle we slaughtered. She was up until near midnight for a week straight."

A familiar pang of guilt pressed in James's chest. He'd been so focused on the ranch work, on getting the cattle and horses ready for winter, that he hadn't paid enough attention to what was happening inside the house. Mrs. Wang had been like a favorite aunt—or maybe a mother—his entire life. He had to do a better job watching over her.

"So what are you thinking?" Robert settled back in his chair, arms crossed, gaze steady. "Hire someone from town?"

"That's the problem." Enoch ran a hand through his dark hair. "There's no one available in Walnut Springs. The few women who might be suitable are already spoken for or have their own families to tend."

"We could put out word farther south." Robert had that thoughtful expression he wore when his mind was calculating a problem. "Maybe someone in Helena would be willing to come up here."

James's mind began to race, an idea forming so quickly it nearly took his breath away. Rose. Sweet Rose, with her gentle hands and kind heart who used to help Mrs. Wang in the kitchen when they were children. Rose, who'd disappeared from his life when he was nine, leaving nothing but an ache that had never quite healed.

He cleared his throat. "I might know of someone."

Three pairs of eyes turned to James with varying degrees of surprise. Enoch's dark brows drew together. "Who?"

James cleared his throat, suddenly feeling like that nine-year-old boy again, trying to explain why Rose mattered so much. "Rose Prescott. You remember her—she and her mother came from England with us and lived here for a while before Mother passed."

"Rose?" Enoch's face lit up with recognition. "Little Rose with the red hair who used to sing when she worked with Mrs. Wang?"

"That's her." Warmth spread through his chest at the memory. Her voice had such a soothing quality, he'd wanted to listen to it for hours. "She'd be perfect for this. She already knows the house, knows our family..."

"James." Enoch's voice carried a note of gentle warning. "That was eleven years ago. She's not a child anymore, and from what I recall, she and her mother left rather suddenly."

"I know where she is." He almost regretted the admission when all three brothers stared at him with renewed interest.

"You do?" Thomas leaned forward. "How?"

James shifted in his chair. "Virginia City. She's...a singer there. Goes by Ruby Starling now. I saw an advertisement in the newspaper for her musical performances."

The hush stretched between them like a tight rope.

Robert spoke first, his gaze studying James. "You've been keeping track of her."

It wasn't a question, and the weight of his brothers' scrutiny pressed in around him. "Not keeping track, exactly. Just...I heard about this singer, Ruby Starling, and something about the name struck me. Then I saw an advertisement in the Virginia City paper with a sketch of her." The jolt of recognition when he'd seen that familiar smile staring back at him from the newsprint had been almost jarring. "It was definitely her."

Enoch studied him with those piercing blue eyes that seemed to see straight through to a man's soul. "Virginia City's a rough place, James. If she's performing there…"

"She's making an honest living." His tone came sharper than he'd meant it to. "Rose would never—" He caught himself. He sounded too defensive. "Look, I'm just saying she might welcome a change. Performing can't be easy work."

Thomas whistled low. "You want to bring a saloon singer up here to help Mrs. Wang?"

Heat flared through him. "She's not a saloon singer." And why did his brothers keep insinuating she was? "She sings in a theater there. Rose is a respectable woman who happens to have a beautiful voice. And she's family—or close enough."

Robert's brows lifted. "Even if she'd be willing to leave Virginia City, why would she want to come back here? If she's performing, she's probably making good money. Better than what we would pay for household help."

James's gut twisted at that very logical statement. Perhaps he could kick in more funds from his portion of the ranch proceeds. "Money isn't everything, Robert. Maybe she'd welcome the chance to be somewhere…" He paused, searching for the right words. "Somewhere she belongs."

"You're assuming a lot about what she wants," Enoch said quietly. "About what her life is like now."

The weight of truth in his brother's words settled like a load of rocks on his shoulders. He *was* assuming. He'd been assuming for years that Rose might want to hear from him, that she might miss what they'd shared here before her mother took her away. The unanswered letters he'd sent through the years were proof enough of how wrong his assumptions might be.

"Besides," Thomas added, "if she's performing under a stage

name, she might not want her past following her. Some people leave for a reason."

James clenched his jaw. "She didn't leave by choice. She was a child. Her mother made that decision."

"And now she's a grown woman who can make her own choices." Robert eyed him. "Including choosing not to return."

The logic was sound, but it did nothing to squelch the restless energy building in James's chest. He'd spent too many years wondering about Rose, too many nights staring at the stars and remembering the sound of her laughter echoing through these rooms. What kind of life had she built for herself? Was she happy? Did she ever think of their childhood together, or had she put all of that behind her? Put him and his family out of her mind?

At last, he sighed. "Maybe she wouldn't. But it can't hurt to ask. The worst she can do is say no."

Enoch was silent for a long moment, his gaze fixed on something beyond the window. When he spoke, his tone was gentle. "If you want to reach out to her, James, you have my blessing. We'd all love to have Rose back if she's willing." He looked around the table at his other brothers, who nodded in agreement. "But don't get your hopes too high. People change. Circumstances change."

"I know." But even as he said it, a spark of hope kindled in his chest. Just the possibility of seeing Rose again, of hearing her songs fill these rooms once more, made something inside him come alive.

The scrape of chairs against the wood floor broke the stillness as his brothers pushed back from the table.

"Well then." Enoch stood and stretched his arms above his head. "I suppose we have our answer. At least a plan to try."

Thomas clapped James on the shoulder as he passed. "Good luck, brother. I hope she says yes."

Robert lingered a moment longer, his expression thoughtful.

"Just remember what Enoch said. Don't build this up too much in your mind."

James dipped his chin, though his pulse had already quickened with possibility. "I'll be careful."

While his brothers headed outside, he climbed the stairs to his room. The familiar creak of the seventh step, the way the afternoon light slanted through the hallway window—everything felt different now, charged with the potential of change.

His room faced west toward the mountains, and he stood at the window for a moment, watching the peaks catch the late afternoon sun. Somewhere beyond those mountains, Rose was living a life he knew nothing about.

He settled at his small writing desk, pulling out a sheet of paper and his pen. But as the nib hovered over the blank page, doubt crept in.

How exactly did a man reach out to someone who'd been ignoring his letters for years?

The stark reality of those unanswered notes hit him like a cold mountain wind. A host of letters over the years—carefully crafted, full of memories and updates on his family and gentle inquiries about her well-being. Letters that had vanished into silence as complete as a winter snowfall.

If Rose wouldn't respond to James Balfour writing to her directly, perhaps she'd respond to something else entirely.

A new idea began to form, one that made his chest tighten with both excitement and guilt. What if it wasn't a letter at all?

The advertisement section of the Virginia City paper—he'd seen plenty of notices there for employment opportunities, respectable positions that drew responses from people seeking honest work.

He pulled out a fresh sheet of paper and dipped his pen in ink.

*Seeking experienced woman for household management position.*

He paused. Too formal. Rose would completely ignore that. He marked through the words and started again.

*Seeking Respectable Woman for Household Position*

*Household assistant needed for established Montana ranch family. Experience with cooking, cleaning, and general domestic duties helpful but not required. Suitable for woman seeking change from mining town life to peaceful mountain ranch.*

*Position includes room and board in comfortable accommodations, plus generous wages. Duties to include cooking assistance, general housekeeping, and companionship for female family members. Remote location requires commitment through winter months.*

He studied the words, imagining Rose reading them in some Virginia City boarding house or theater. Would she be curious enough to respond? Would the promise of mountains and peace appeal to someone who'd been performing in the rough-and-tumble world of a mining town?

He added one more line:

*Reply to Telegraph Office, Walnut Springs, Montana Territory.*

Would she think it odd for the correspondence to be held at the telegraph office? It was clear that he wanted to remain anonymous, but maybe that wasn't uncommon for general advertisements like this that might receive a horde of responses.

He glanced over the missive once more. This would do. He'd ride to town tomorrow morning to send the message to the Virginia City newspaper. That would be the *only* town he advertised in.

Then he'd give a week to wait for Rose's response. If she didn't answer, he'd ride to Virginia City and plead his case in person.

Certainly she couldn't resist a bit of the Balfour charm from her oldest friend.

He could only pray one of these steps would work. Something inside him had come to life with the thought of Rose back in his life, and he wouldn't give up this dream again.

Not like he'd been forced to the first time she left.

# CHAPTER 2

Rose Prescott let her hands fall to her sides as her final note faded into the rafters. That familiar bone-deep ache settled in her chest as applause rippled through the singing hall, a large room added to the back of Murphy's Saloon. Men clustered around the small tables, raised their glasses, and called for more, but she was already edging toward the narrow doorway leading to the backstage area.

"That's all for tonight, gentlemen." She kept her voice warm enough to satisfy, but distant, as always.

The emerald silk dress her stepfather insisted she wear clung to her skin, and she had to work to draw breath in the thick air, heavy with the stench of cigars and spilled whiskey.

She slipped behind the curtain. Her slippers made no sound on the warped boards. The hallway back here was cooler, at least, though the sounds of the saloon—raucous laughter, the clink of glasses, the occasional crash of furniture—followed her like ghosts.

"Ruby."

She tensed as Vincent Dunhill's voice cut through her brief moment of peace like a knife blade. When she turned, he leaned against the wall, his bulk blocking most of the dim light from the oil lamp mounted nearby.

Even in the shadows, his pale eyes glinted.

"The take was good tonight." He straightened, and at nearly six feet, he loomed over her.

"Better than last week. That new song you've been working on—the melancholy one about lost love—they ate it up."

Rose nodded, though something cold twisted in her stomach at his satisfied tone. Vincent always spoke of her performances like a merchant discussing his most profitable goods. "I'm glad it pleased them."

"Pleased them?" His laugh was low and calculating. "Ruby, my dear, you had half those men ready to weep into their whiskey. That's not just pleasing—that's artistry." He reached out to adjust a wayward curl that had escaped her carefully arranged hair, and she forced herself not to flinch. Having his hand so close to her tightened every muscle in her body. "Your mother would be proud."

The mention of Mama sent a familiar pang through her chest. Margaret Prescott had been dead four years now, but Vincent still wielded her memory like a weapon when it suited him.

"I'm tired, Vincent. May I retire for the evening?"

"Of course, of course." But his hand settled on her shoulder, fingers pressing just firmly enough to remind her who held the power between them. "Though I did want to discuss expanding your repertoire. Perhaps something a bit more…spirited for the weekend crowds."

Rose's throat tightened. She knew what he meant by spirited —songs that would encourage the men to drink more, stay longer, spend more money. Songs that would chip away another piece of her dignity.

She was tired. Soul-weary tired in a way that had nothing to do with the late hour and everything to do with the weight of the twenty-year contract that bound her to this life.

"Good night, Vincent."

He stepped aside to let her pass, but the burn of his gaze followed her down the narrow hallway to her dressing room. The door stuck slightly—it always did in the damp mountain air —and she had to put her shoulder against it to get it open.

The small space barely contained a washstand, a cracked mirror, and a trunk for her costumes. But it was hers, the only place in Virginia City where she could drop the mask of Ruby Starling and simply be Rose Prescott again.

She sank onto the single wooden chair and unpinned her hair, letting the auburn waves fall around her shoulders. In the mirror's reflection, the weariness in her own green eyes stared back at her. Her smile had become a practiced thing that never quite reached them anymore.

Sixteen years left. The contract stretched ahead of her like a prison sentence, payment for her mother's medical bills and funeral expenses. Vincent had been so generous, so under-standing when Mama lay dying. He'd taken care of everything— the doctors, the medicines, the burial plot. All Rose had to do was sign her name and promise to perform until the debt was paid.

She'd been fifteen and desperate. Now she was twenty, and the debt seemed to grow rather than shrink with each passing month.

She pulled out the day-old copy of the *Virginia City Enterprise* that someone had left behind in the saloon. She often read the advertisements, though she couldn't say why. Perhaps it was the glimpse they offered into other lives, other possibilities.

Her gaze drifted over notices for mining equipment, cattle for sale, and rooms to let. Then a small advertisement near the bottom of the page snagged her attention:

*Seeking Respectable Woman for Household Position*

She read the words advertising the job of household assistant twice, then a third time, her heart beating faster. It sounded like a dream…or an echo from the past. A peaceful mountain ranch. Away from the smoke and noise and calculating eyes. Away from Vincent.

But even as hope flickered to life in her chest, reality crashed over her like snowy water. The contract. Vincent would never let her leave. And he had contacts everywhere. He would find her and drag her back. Then he'd make her pay for ever thinking she could best him.

Still, her fingers traced the words *peaceful mountain ranch.* What would it be like to wake up to clean mountain air instead of the stale smoke of the saloon? To spend her days helping with honest work instead of performing for strangers who saw only what they wanted to see? Singing in front of men who saw her as a thing to enjoy instead of a person.

Walnut Springs. The name stirred something in her memory, though she couldn't place what.

She couldn't remember the name of the town nearest the Balfour ranch, but might Walnut Springs be it?

Surely not. The Montana Territory was so vast—it could be anywhere. Perhaps she'd heard a drunken miner mention the name.

She folded the newspaper and tucked it into her trunk beneath her spare chemise. Just having it there, hidden away like a secret, made something flutter in her chest that she hadn't felt in months. Years even.

Hope, perhaps. Or maybe only the desperate craving for something different.

She stood and moved to the small window, pushing aside the faded curtain to look out at the night. Virginia City sprawled below in a maze of flickering lights and shadows, the constant noise of the saloons echoing even at this late hour.

Somewhere beyond those hills lay ranch country—wide open spaces where a person could breathe freely. She barely remembered what that felt like. She and her mother had moved here when she was nine, and she had so few memories from before.

But sometimes, in dreams, she remembered sunshine streaming through tall windows and the sound of laughter echoing through spacious rooms. A kitchen that smelled of fresh bread and herbs, not stale beer and tobacco. Strong hands teaching her to knead dough, and a boy with dark hair who used to make her laugh until her sides ached.

Those memories felt like someone else's life now, soft and golden and impossibly distant.

A place she could never return.

Rose pressed her forehead against the cool glass. The advertisement would be for a different ranch, so maybe…

But she couldn't respond. Of course she couldn't.

The contract felt like heavy chains around her wrists, binding her to this smoky world where she was nothing more than Vincent's investment.

Yet if she could find a way to get free of Vincent. If she could line up work before she attempted escape…

Did she dare?

She pressed her palm against the cold pane. Once upon a time, she'd believed God watched over her. That he cared about a little girl and her mother who'd had to leave the safe, happy ranch and go on an adventure to the city.

But He hadn't answered when Mama's breath grew thin and rattling. He hadn't answered when Vincent's contract chained her. Perhaps heaven helped women who had earned it somehow —good women, strong women. Not the sort who sang to keep a man's ledger balanced.

"Please," she whispered before she could stop herself. The word felt foolish in the smoky dark. "If You see me—if You still do—let me out." Only silence followed.

She would have to find her own way.

She turned back to the room and pulled out the newspaper again, smoothing the creases with trembling fingers.

What harm could there be in simply writing a telegram? Not to accept the position—she couldn't do that, not without knowing more—but perhaps simply to inquire. To imagine, for a few precious moments, what it might be like to have choices again.

She pulled out a sheet of writing paper from the small supply she'd horded away. Her pen hovered over the blank page as she considered her words.

*To Telegraph Office, Walnut Springs, Montana Territory:*

*INQUIRING ABOUT HOUSEHOLD POSITION ON RANCH STOP EXPERIENCED WITH HOUSEKEEPING STOP PLEASE RESPOND WITH STARTING DATE IF POSITION STILL AVAIL-ABLE STOP REPLIES TO VIRGINIA CITY TELEGRAPH OFFICE ATTENTION MISS R P FULL STOP*

She stared at the words, her heart hammering. Miss R. Prescott—not Ruby Starling. No one at the telegraph office knew her by that name, so the reply would sit until she came to fetch it. And using her real name felt like shedding a costume, like stepping out from behind the emerald silk and stage lights into something true.

Was she exaggerating by saying she had experience with housekeeping? She kept her own room well, and she and Mama had always cooked for themselves in the little stove downstairs beneath their rooms. She could learn quickly, so surely she'd be able to pick up any other skills needed.

Tomorrow she would find a way to slip to the telegraph office to send this during the afternoon, when Vincent was busy with his other business ventures. She had enough coins saved from the tips customers sometimes pressed into her hand— money Vincent didn't know about— hidden away in the false bottom of her jewelry box.

But what if Vincent found out? What if he intercepted the reply? The telegraph office wasn't far from Murphy's, and Vincent had friends everywhere in Virginia City. Men who owed him favors, who would tell him if Rose Prescott started receiving mysterious messages.

She crumpled the paper and tossed it toward the small waste basket, but it missed and landed on the floor beside her chair. The sight of her initials, written in her own careful script, lying crumpled and discarded made something fierce rise up in her chest.

She was tired of being afraid. Tired of Vincent's watchful eyes and calculating smiles. Tired of singing other people's sorrows while her own dreams withered away like flowers in a drought.

Rose smoothed out the telegram and read it once more. The words looked small and uncertain on the page, but they represented something larger—the first step toward a life that might be her saving grace.

# CHAPTER 3

The responding telegram arrived two days later.

Rose stood in the narrow alley behind Murphy's Saloon, her hands trembling as she unfolded the response from Walnut Springs. The morning air carried the scent of pine from the surrounding mountains, but she barely noticed, her entire attention focused on the message:

*POSITION AVAILABLE IMMEDIATELY STOP ROOM AND BOARD PROVIDED STOP WAGES FIFTEEN DOLLARS MONTHLY STOP REPLY WITH ARRIVAL DATE IF INTER-ESTED STOP MEET AT WALNUT SPRINGS CAFE FULL STOP*

Fifteen dollars. More than she'd seen in years. But it was the word *immediately* that made her pulse quicken—as though whoever had placed the advertisement understood that some situations required swift escape.

She read the telegram three more times, committing each word to memory. No mention of a family name, no specific details about the ranch's location beyond Walnut Springs.

The anonymity should possibly concern her, but instead it

felt like Providence. If she didn't know who was offering her this lifeline, Vincent couldn't discover it either.

"Ruby?"

Vincent's voice from the saloon's back door made her jump. She quickly folded the telegram and slipped it into her skirt pocket, her heart hammering against her ribs.

"Just working to memorize that new song." She forced lightness into her tone.

"Come inside. We need to discuss tonight's performance."

She followed him back into the dim interior, but her mind remained fixed on those precious words: *Position available immediately*. The telegram felt warm against her leg through the fabric of her pocket, like a secret flame Vincent couldn't extinguish.

"I've been thinking about that new arrangement," Vincent was saying as they walked through the narrow hallway. "Something with more...appeal for the gentlemen who frequent the back tables."

Rose made the appropriate sounds of agreement, but her thoughts already raced ahead to practicalities. She'd studied the map in the telegraph office, the one with the stage routes drawn in dark lines. She'd have to get off in Butte and find other transportation to the little town of Walnut Springs. That might be better though. Harder for Vincent to track her.

The stagecoach to Butte left twice weekly—Tuesdays and Saturdays. Today was Thursday, which meant she had two days to plan her escape if she chose Saturday's departure. She had enough to cover the cost of the stage, but barely more for the remaining travel. She would need to bring food to eat along the way.

Two days to gather her courage and what few belongings she could carry without arousing suspicion.

"Ruby? Are you listening?"

She blinked, focusing on Vincent's pale eyes. "Of course. The new arrangement."

"Good." His smile didn't reach his eyes. "I've also had an inquiry about a private performance. A wealthy mining investor, new to Virginia City. The compensation would be...substantial."

Something cold settled in Rose's stomach. Vincent's private performances had grown more frequent lately, and more lucrative. They also required her to sing in drawing rooms and private dining halls where the audience was smaller, more intimate, and where the line between performer and entertainment grew dangerously thin.

The men often wanted to wrap an arm around her. Have her sit on their lap and sing to them. Or share a drink with them. She hated that vile stuff. Hated every retched part of it—the stench, the way it loosened men's tongues and freed their hands. Made them either angry or far too pushy.

She forced down the bile that rose at just the thought. "When?"

"Saturday afternoon. Nothing too demanding—an hour or two of your most popular songs." Vincent's hand settled on her shoulder again, that familiar weight of ownership. "Appearances like this are stated in your contract."

She forced herself to nod. "I know."

She had to leave on Saturday's stage. Escape.

As soon as she reached her room, she drafted a telegram to send back to Walnut Springs.

*ARRIVING SUNDAY MORNING STAGE IN BUTTE STOP SHOULD REACH WS MONDAY STOP WILL MEET IN CAFÉ MONDAY NOON STOP WILL WEAR HAT WITH RED FEATHER STOP SIGNED R P FULL STOP*

The red feather—she wore it with the ruby dress Vincent

sometimes insisted on. It would be distinctive enough without looking gaudy. Hopefully.

She inhaled a deep breath and released it. Two days. She had to remain calm so Vincent didn't suspect anything.

No matter what, she couldn't let him follow her. She had no doubt he'd look for her. And if he found her, there was no telling how he'd make her pay for daring to defy him.

# CHAPTER 4

The streets of Butte City teemed with more desperate souls than James remembered from the last time he'd been here three years ago. He'd forgotten how rough mining towns could be.

He eased his wagon along the muddy ruts, eyeing the men slouched against doorways or gathered in knots near the saloons. The mining boom had drawn fortune-seekers from every corner of the country, and most of them looked like they'd sell their own mothers for a decent claim.

This was no place for a woman alone.

Just picturing Rose out here, picking her way through these streets with no one to watch her back, set his jaw tight. He'd known there would be little reliable transport she could find from here to Walnut Springs. The stage line didn't run that far into the mountains. And the freight wagons that did were hardly meant for a lady. There hadn't been time to respond to her last telegram. He'd just come knowing she'd need help.

A painted sign in the window of Loeser's Dry Goods read *Stage Stop Inside*. He reined his team to a halt before the building.

The horses stamped at the muck, tossing their heads, eager to be away from the racket and press of bodies. He didn't blame them.

The bell over the door jingled as he stepped in. He took in the cramped space, barrels of flour stacked beside bolts of calico.

And then he saw her.

Even with her back turned, it had to be Rose. That auburn hair, not so bright as the coppery tangle she'd worn as a child, was gathered beneath a plain traveling hat, a single red feather tucked into the band. Her dress was a simple blue, the skirt dulled by dust but still somehow refined. When she shifted, he caught the profile that had haunted his sleep for years.

She was more beautiful than he remembered, more than he'd let himself imagine. No longer the skinny girl with freckles and grass stains on her pinafore. In her place stood a woman, grown and graceful. The gentle curve of her cheek, the line of her neck above the collar—it left him breathless.

She spoke to a grizzled man in worn buckskins, her voice low and musical even in conversation. James couldn't make out the words, but that voice…

*…that voice.*

It still carried the same sweet cadence that had lulled him to sleep on sunny days during those long-ago summers at the ranch.

He moved closer, finally catching her words.

"—to Walnut Springs."

The man she spoke to scratched his beard and answered with a rough voice. "Walnut Springs, eh? That's a fair piece into the mountains. I could get you as far as Deer Lodge. That's half the distance, maybe. Eight dollars, and you'd be riding in the back of a freight wagon, with supplies for the mining camps."

Her shoulders stiffened. "Eight dollars? For halfway?"

"Take it or leave it, lady. Ain't nobody else heading that direction for another week, maybe two."

James stepped forward before he could second-guess himself. "Excuse me, miss. I couldn't help overhearing. I'm headed to Walnut Springs myself—could give you a ride for nothing. All the way there."

Rose turned, and when those green eyes met his, he braced himself for recognition. Up close, she was even more striking—those familiar freckles still dusted her nose, though fainter now, and her skin had the pale quality of someone who spent her days indoors. But it was her expression that caught him off guard. Wariness flickered across her features, quick as a bird taking flight.

"That's very kind of you, Mr...?"

"James."

She showed no sign of knowing him, not even after hearing his name. No warmth chased away that careful distance in her voice. She simply looked at him with polite hesitation, as though he were any stranger offering assistance.

The grizzled man shrugged and spat into a nearby spittoon. "Suit yourself, miss. Makes no difference to me."

Rose hesitated, her gloved hands fidgeting with the straps of her traveling bag. "I don't wish to impose—"

"No imposition. I've got a comfortable wagon that won't be overloaded, and the weather looks fair." James kept his tone easy, though his heart beat fast enough to power a mill wheel. "Safer than traveling with freight wagons, I'd wager."

Still she hesitated, and something like calculation entered her eyes. Like she was weighing the risk of accepting help from a stranger against the alternatives Butte had to offer.

Finally, she nodded, though her smile remained cautious. "Very well. Thank you, Mr. James."

He wanted to correct her—to tell her his full name, to see if that might stir a memory—but something held him back. Perhaps it was the careful way she braced herself, like she'd learned not to trust too quickly. Or perhaps not trust at all. What had happened to her these past eleven years?

"My wagon's just outside." He nodded toward the door. "We can load your things and head out."

"This is all I have." She lifted her carpet bag.

He kept from raising his brows and motioned for her to precede him to the exit.

They made their way outside, where his wagon waited between two freight haulers. He cupped her elbow to help her up onto the bench seat, and even through the fabric of her traveling dress, she was so delicate—all bird bones and careful grace.

Once they were settled and he guided the team through the crowded streets, she spoke. "I'm Rose. Rose Prescott."

At least she still used her real name. That had to mean something. "Pleased to meet you, Miss Prescott."

He guided the horses around a particularly deep rut, stealing glances at her profile. The years had refined her features, but he could still see traces of the girl who used to race him through the meadows behind the ranch house. The stubborn set of her chin when she was determined about something. The way she tucked a strand of hair behind her ear when she was thinking.

"Are you from Walnut Springs?" She gripped the handles of her bag like it might slide out of the wagon.

"Near there. My family has a ranch in the mountains." He kept his voice casual, though every word felt loaded with significance. "What brings you there, if you don't mind my asking?"

"Employment." The single word carried a finality that discouraged further questions. She really must not have even an inkling of who he was.

Maybe he shouldn't be surprised. She'd not expect her new employer to pick her up in Butte. And she still didn't know the Balfour family had placed the advertisement. So she wouldn't be looking for her old friend.

Yet still... He'd have known Rose anywhere. Right? Maybe he'd changed more than she had.

They rode in silence for a while as the buildings of Butte City gave way to rolling hills dotted with scrub pine. The road wound upward, and he gave the animals enough rein to set their own pace on the steady climb. Rose sat straight-backed beside him, her traveling bag clutched in her lap like armor.

The horses settled into a steady rhythm, and finally she seemed to relax a little, though she still held herself with that careful reserve.

He stole an occasional glance at her—those same delicate fingers that used to help Mrs. Wang knead bread dough, now gloved in worn leather that had seen better days. Everything about her spoke of genteel poverty, of someone who'd learned to make do with less while maintaining her dignity.

Her eyes softened when they passed a meadow dotted with wildflowers. And when the road carried them through trees again, she lifted her face to the sun filtering through the pine boughs.

"It's beautiful country." She spoke softly, and something in her voice made him think she'd been starved for beauty.

"It is." He wanted to say more—wanted to tell her about the mornings when mist rose from the valleys like prayers, about the way the mountains looked when they wore their first snow. Instead, he tried for something casual. "Have you spent much time in mountain country?"

"Some." She fell quiet again, like she'd revealed more than she intended.

Her silence weighed heavy between them. She parceled out information like it was precious currency. The Rose he remembered had been full of chatter, spinning stories about the clouds and asking endless questions about everything from why horses slept standing up to whether angels could fly faster than birds.

This Rose held her words close, and it made his chest ache.

They'd been traveling for nearly an hour when he could stand it no more. He pulled the wagon to a stop beside a grove of aspens.

Rose glanced around, and a flicker of wariness crossed her features.

He turned on the bench to face her fully. He had to force himself not to be distracted by the delicate line of her jaw, the way her green eyes reflected the dappled light. "Rose." Her name felt like coming home. "You don't remember me at all, do you?"

Her eyes went wide, and for a heartbeat, something like fear flashed across her face. She shifted on the bench seat, her grip tightening on her bag.

"Should I?" Her voice held the slightest tremor, like a ripple through still water.

"James Balfour." He watched her face as he spoke the name, searching for some spark of recognition, for the warmth he remembered from long ago. "You and your mother lived at our ranch when we were kids. You came from England with us."

The color drained from her cheeks, and she swayed a little where she sat. Her lips parted, but no sound came. When she found her voice, it came out thin, barely more than a breath. "Jamie?"

The old nickname twisted something deep in his chest. "Yes."

She stared at him, as if she couldn't quite believe he was real, her green eyes searching his face. He saw the moment it truly struck her—the way her expression shifted, first wary, then wonder, then something close to panic.

"Oh." The single word escaped her lips like a prayer—or a curse—he couldn't tell which. Her face cycled through a dozen emotions—surprise, recognition, something that looked almost like joy before it shuttered behind that careful reserve again. "I suppose I should call you Lord Balfour. I...I didn't recognize you. You're so..." She gestured vaguely at him, then dropped her hand. "Different."

"Eleven years will do that." He kept his voice gentle, though his heart battered against his ribs. "And call me James. My brothers and I decided a long time ago not to use our titles here."

She studied him, as though searching out the reasons for that choice. He'd gladly tell her—they weren't deep or any great secret. Maybe in England his father was the Duke of Clarence, a powerful member of the House of Parliament and distant cousin of Queen Victoria. But here in American lands, he was just a regular person, liked and respected for what he did, not his lineage. All his brothers felt the same.

But Rose didn't ask. Instead, she looked away, staring at the aspens like they might offer escape. "Thank you for offering me a ride." She glanced back with a tight smile. "I'm glad it's you and not a stranger."

She didn't *look* particularly glad. Not with the pressed line of her mouth.

What had he done to make her dislike him? She and her mother had left so many years ago, but he'd never been aware of saying or doing anything to hurt her. Of course, his days had been dark during that time, what with Mother's passing. Then with Rose leaving too… The entire year felt like a murky fog.

Something cold settled in his gut now as he watched her not meet his gaze. This wasn't the reunion he'd imagined during all those sleepless nights.

He'd thought his letters must not have reached her. But maybe she really didn't ever want to see him or his family again. Had her mother turned her against them? His memories of Mrs. Prescott were only pleasant. She'd been his own mother's best friend, as well as her lady's maid.

He had to tell Rose the job she came for was with his family, though he hated the thought of her response. If she harbored ill feelings toward the Balfours, she might not be willing to work for them. Yet there was no sense in riding farther only to turn back if she decided not to take the position.

"Rose." He kept his voice careful, gentle. "The job you're traveling to—it's with my family. At our ranch."

Her face went perfectly still, like a deer that just caught the scent of a hunter. "Your family?"

"We need help for Mrs. Wang—she's getting on in years, and with my sister-in-law expecting…" He let the words trail off, watching the way Rose's grip tightened on her bag. "We'd love for you to come home."

"Home." She repeated the word as though it were foreign on her tongue. Something flicked in her eyes—longing, perhaps, or pain. "I see."

The flatness in her voice made his chest tighten even more. He held his breath, torn between hoping she'd stay and fearing what it might mean if she did.

This wasn't the eager, trusting girl who used to follow him through the meadows. This Rose looked like she might bolt at any sudden movement.

"Mrs. Wang is still there?" Something shifted in her voice— the first genuine warmth since she'd spoken his childhood name.

"Still there. Still keeping us all straight." He managed a smile. "She's asked about you through the years. Wondered what became of Margaret Prescott's little songbird."

For a moment, her careful mask slipped. Grief welled in her eyes, and something deeper—a longing so sharp it made his chest ache.

"Mama died a few years ago." The words came out lifeless, practiced, like she'd had to say them too many times.

"I'm sorry." The statement felt so inadequate, but he meant it. "She was a good woman. My mother's dearest friend."

Rose nodded stiffly, looking away toward the mountains. "She was."

After a moment, her gaze dropped to her hands. "Mrs. Wang...she taught me to make her special dumplings. Does she still serve them?"

"She does." A spark of hope lit inside him at the softening in Rose's voice. "They're my favorites."

They sat in silence, the aspens rustling overhead. A hawk circled high above the meadow, riding the mountain wind with lazy grace.

He had to give her an out, in case that's what she truly wanted. He wouldn't force her to come. "If you don't want to take the position, I can drive you back to Butte. Or arrange passage wherever you'd rather go. No questions asked."

Rose stayed quiet so long, it seemed she might not answer. When she finally spoke, her voice came out barely audible. "What would the work entail? Exactly?"

"Helping Mrs. Wang with the cooking, the cleaning. Some mending, perhaps. Keeping my sister-in-law company— Mandie, Enoch's wife. She gets lonely with the men out working the ranch all day." He paused. "Nothing you haven't done before, from what I remember."

"And your brothers? Are they all still there?"

He nodded. "Enoch, Robert, and Thomas. Enoch is married, of course, and they're expecting a babe in another month or so." He studied her profile, the ache rising in his throat at this next part. Both for him, and for her, hearing the news fresh. "Will passed last year. An accident with one of the colts in training."

That still felt surreal to say. Will had been so strong and capable. To think he was gone...forever...

Rose gasped, and she spun back to him as her hand moved to cover her mouth. "Will? Oh, Jamie." The old nickname slipped out again, and with it came another crack in her careful composure. "I'm so sorry. He was so... He was always so kind to me."

This was the Rose he remembered—the one whose heart

broke for others' pain, who'd once cried when they found a baby bird fallen from its nest.

He nodded. "He would have been glad to see you again. They all will be."

She remained quiet another long moment, her fingers worrying the edge of her glove. When she spoke again, her voice had regained that careful control. "The position—it would include room and board?"

"Your own room, the same one you and your mother shared. Meals with the family."

Emotions played across her features—hope warring with fear, longing battling with some deep-seated caution. "Would it be..." She hesitated, then straightened her shoulders, and her tone turned more business-like. "Would it be acceptable if I stayed for a trial period? Two weeks, perhaps? To see if the arrangement suits everyone?"

The tension slipped from his chest. "Of course." He kept the eagerness out of his voice, though his heart already raced ahead to the moment she'd walk through the familiar doors of the ranch house. "And if it doesn't work out, I'll personally see you get safe passage back to...wherever you'd like to go."

She nodded, though he caught the flicker of something— gratitude, perhaps, or simply relief—before she looked away to the mountains again. "Then I accept. For two weeks."

"Good." He turned back to the horses, releasing the brake. "If we push, we should reach the ranch by nightfall."

# CHAPTER 5

The morning brought no escape from the reckoning Rose had been dreading since the moment she'd recognized Lord James Balfour on that dusty road.

Except not *Lord* Balfour. Just…James. It felt odd not thinking of them as gentry. Her mother had called him Master James most of the time.

Will had been the heir apparent, bearing his father's lesser title—the earl of something, if she remembered correctly—until he would take over the dukedom on their father's death. Enoch had a different title, passed through their mother. The Baron of Stafford, or something close to that.

If Will was gone, did that mean Enoch was now the earl? And James a baron? The titles of the peerage had always been a bit convoluted in her mind, probably because they'd left England when she was four. No matter how the inherited designations had changed with Will's death, the fact remained—the Balfour family were peers of the realm.

And she would be one of their servants.

They'd reached the ranch so late last night, everyone else had already been asleep. For her part, even after collapsing into the familiar bed of her childhood, she'd barely slept. So many memories she'd long-since forgotten surfaced like spring wildflowers pushing through snow.

How many times had she dreamed of James coming to rescue her in Virginia City? It'd been a hopeless wish. Something she'd known couldn't come true. James hadn't known where she was. And in truth, she'd only been the help. A servant. Why would he come after her?

She'd prayed so many times too. If James wouldn't save her, maybe God would. She'd sent up desperate, whispered pleas in the dark. *Please let me go home. Please let someone find me. Please let this end.*

She'd stopped praying eventually, when the silence from heaven grew too heavy. Too disappointing.

But somehow, she'd made it back to the Balfour ranch. Maybe—just maybe—some of those prayers had been heard after all.

Now, she stood hiding outside the dining room. She had to face them all—the brothers who'd once been her dearest friends. Before her mother whisked her away with hushed words about never being welcome here again.

She smoothed her blue skirt, the only other dress she'd managed to squeeze into her bag, and stepped into the dining room.

Conversation died as though someone dropped a curtain over the scene. Five pairs of eyes turned toward her—Enoch's piercing blue gaze, Robert's gentle brown eyes, Thomas's curious stare, and James's green eyes that seemed to search her face for something she wasn't sure she could give.

A woman she didn't recognize sat beside Enoch, her condition unmistakable, even seated. One hand rested protectively over her rounded belly.

"Rose!" Mrs. Wang's voice cut through the stillness as the

elderly Chinese woman hurried from the kitchen, wiping her hands on her apron. "Dear child, let me look at you."

Suddenly everyone was rising from their chairs, moving toward her with grins and words piled on top of each other.

Mrs. Wang reached Rose first, taking her hands in those dear, weathered ones. "Still so beautiful like your mama." Her dark eyes glistened. "But too thin, child. We'll fix that."

"Mrs. Wang." The burning in her eyes and throat made Rose's voice crack. Mrs. Wang looked older, her black hair now mixed with a great deal of silver, but her smile hadn't changed a bit—warm and encompassing, like being wrapped in a quilt fresh from the sunshine.

"Rose." Enoch stepped forward. He'd changed so much. As a boy, he'd been tall and lanky, yet this man bore broad shoulders and a quiet, commanding presence. When he smiled, though, she caught a glimpse of the brother who'd once taught her to skip stones across the creek. "Welcome home."

*Home.* That word again, the one that made her chest tighten with equal parts longing and fear.

Robert appeared at her other side, his gentle eyes crinkling with genuine pleasure. "It's been far too long, Rose. You look well."

"Thank you." Yet were his words actually true? The mirror in her room this morning had shown her a woman haunted, with shadows around her eyes and a wariness etched into her bones.

Thomas, taller now but still bearing that mischievous glint his eyes had held even as a tot, bounded forward with the same enthusiasm as back then. "Rose! I can't believe you're really here. Wait until you see how much the ranch has grown—"

"Thomas." James's voice carried a gentle warning. "Let her breathe."

The woman, heavy with child, approached, one hand supporting her back.

She was lovely, with dark hair and warm brown eyes that

held a quiet intelligence. "I'm Mandie, Enoch's wife." Her smile was gentle, welcoming. "We're so glad you're here. I've heard so much about you."

Heat crept up her neck. What exactly had they said? That she'd run away without a word? "It's a pleasure to meet you, Mrs. Balfour. Congratulations on your coming addition." Should she have said *Lady Balfour*? Just because the brothers didn't want their titles used didn't mean this woman was just as unpretentious.

"Call me Mandie, please." Her hand moved protectively over her belly. "And thank you. We're very excited, though I confess I'm grateful you're here to help Bea. I've been feeling rather useless lately."

"Nonsense." Mrs. Wang waved the comment away. "Enough standing around. Rose needs breakfast, and this baby needs its mama sitting down."

She bustled toward Rose, taking her elbow with gentle firmness. "Come, child. Your place is here, between Robert and James."

Rose's stomach clenched at the mention of *her place*, as though eleven years hadn't passed, as though she belonged here now simply because she once had.

But she allowed herself to be guided to the chair, acutely aware of James sitting beside her, his bulk both comforting and unsettling.

Once they'd all sat, Enoch bowed his head and thanked the Lord for bread, for strength to work, for the baby, and for "old friends come home." No flourish. No sermon. Just a few plain words that landed soft as a quilt.

As plates were passed and conversations resumed, it felt like she was caught in a strange suspension between past and present. The dining room looked exactly as she remembered— the same heavy oak furniture, the same view of the mountains through tall windows, even the same chip in the seat of her chair. Yet everything felt different through the lens of her adult eyes, smaller somehow, welcoming in a different way.

"Do you remember"—Enoch buttered a thick slice of Mrs. Wang's fresh bread—"how you used to insist on helping with the morning milking, even though you were afraid of the cows?"

"I was not afraid," Rose protested automatically, then caught herself. The defense had come so naturally. "I was...cautious."

Robert chuckled. "Cautious enough to hide behind James every time Bessie looked at you."

"Bessie was enormous." It was remarkable how easily she fell into the familiar rhythm of their teasing. "And she had very judgmental eyes."

Thomas laughed. "She still does. Though she's gotten lazy in her old age—barely lifts her head when you call her from the pasture now."

"You still have her?" The question slipped out before Rose could stop it.

"Of course, though she's retired now," James said quietly. "Some things are too precious to let go."

The weight of his words settled over the table like morning mist, and heat rose to her cheeks. She focused on her plate, cutting her eggs into precise pieces while the conversation continued around her.

She hadn't expected this warmth, this easy acceptance. Her mother had always spoken of their departure in hushed, urgent tones—how the Balfours would never forgive what had happened. And then, when she was twelve and Vincent began to require her to sing with Mama, Mama had told her what actually had happened to make them leave the Balfours. She'd understood why they couldn't come back here.

She'd always assumed the Balfour family knew the truth and would hate her for it. Was it possible they didn't know?

"Tell us about yourself, Rose," Mandie said gently, setting down her teacup. "What have you been doing these past years?"

The question she'd been dreading. Rose's fork paused halfway to her mouth as six expectant faces turned toward her. "I've been in Virginia City," she said carefully. "I...performed. Singing."

"Singing!" Mrs. Wang clapped her hands together. "I knew it. You always had such a beautiful voice, even as a little one. Remember how you used to sing while you helped me with the washing?"

Rose managed a smile. "I remember."

"Virginia City must have been exciting." Thomas leaned forward. "All those mining fortunes being made and lost. I heard they have theaters there now, real fancy ones."

"Some." She took a small bite to buy herself time. How could she explain the smoky back room of Murphy's Saloon, the calculating eyes of men who saw her as entertainment rather than a person? "It's a...busy place."

Robert spoke in a gentle tone, like he could sense her discomfort. "Well, you'll find it much quieter here. Mrs. Wang, perhaps after breakfast, you could show Rose around? I imagine much has changed."

Gratitude flooded her, and she smiled. "I'd like that very much."

Mrs. Wang beamed. "Yes, yes. New stove, bigger pantry. And I teach you my grandmother's recipe for steamed cabbage—very good for strengthening the blood."

"I'd love to learn it." Truly. The thought of spending her days in the familiar warmth of Mrs. Wang's kitchen, learning recipes instead of dodging unwanted advances, felt like stepping into sunlight after years in the shadows.

"Wonderful." Enoch pushed back from the table, his chair scraping against the wooden floor. "We'll be working on the haying in the north pasture today."

Robert stood as well, but his gaze lingered on Rose with that same gentle consideration his tone held moments ago. "If you need anything at all, don't hesitate to ask. We want you to feel comfortable here."

"Thank you." Her words came out too soft, but the brightness that entered his gaze warmed her insides. Robert possessed a good heart. She could see that from only these few interactions.

After the men filed out, their boots echoing on the wooden floors and their voices carrying back from the hallway, some of the tension eased from her shoulders.

"Rose."

She glanced back to see James lingering in the doorway, his hand resting on the frame. His gaze locked on her, his eyes earnest. "I'm glad you're here."

Then he turned and left before she could respond, leaving her with Mrs. Wang and Mandie—and the tumult of her emotions—in the sudden quiet of the dining room.

# CHAPTER 6

The scythe blade swept through the tall grass, each pass in time with James's pulse—a steady, urgent cadence, edged with something close to worry.

He stopped to check their progress and mop his brow, though the mountain air held a chill that hadn't been there just last week. His brothers worked nearby, silent and intent, their motions fluid, almost spare, as they cut and forked the hay into the wagon. The north pasture stretched ahead, a little more than a quarter cleared now, but winter pressed close behind them, cold and relentless as a wolf on the scent.

Enoch straightened and stared at the work they'd accomplished. "Let's get this load in the shed, then we'll stop to eat a bite." His words formed white clouds, and the lines at the corners of his eyes seemed deeper than usual. They all felt it— the urgency to finish storing all the hay before the first snow. The cattle that would soon need every bit of it to last through a hard winter.

Thomas drove the team toward the shed in the corner of the pasture that they'd built to house the hay. Each field contained such a building, making it easy to fork out hay for the cattle once snow covered the ground.

The four of them worked in silence, stacking the hay high in the shed.

His thoughts kept drifting to the breakfast table, to the way Rose had looked when she'd smiled at Robert—that same warm expression she'd once reserved for James alone. The memory sat in his chest like a stone.

"James." Enoch's voice cut through his brooding. "You're woolgathering."

He blinked. How long had he been holding this same forkful of hay? "Sorry."

Robert stepped past him with his own loaded pitchfork. "Thinking about our houseguest?"

He tightened his jaw. "Thinking about winter. Same as you should be."

"Rose seems to be settling in well." Thomas shucked the hay from his tines and strode back for another load. "Mrs. Wang was beside herself this morning. Haven't seen her that happy in months."

"Good." James tried to keep his voice casual, but something in the way Robert glanced at him suggested he wasn't fooling anyone.

They finished unloading the wagon, then pulled out the food sack Mrs. Wang had packed.

James sat on a fallen log, unwrapping a thick sandwich. The bread was soft enough she must have baked it that morning, then filled it with sliced ham and her pickled vegetables. But his appetite had deserted him somewhere between Rose's careful politeness at breakfast and Robert's knowing looks.

"She remembers more than I expected," Thomas said between bites. "About the ranch, I mean."

"Of course she remembers." The words came out sharper than he'd intended. "She lived here for years."

Enoch studied him with those penetrating blue eyes. "Something troubling you about Rose being here?"

*Everything.* The way she looked through him as though he were a stranger. The careful distance in her voice when she spoke to him. The way she'd brightened when Robert talked to her.

"Nope," he said instead. "Just concerned about the hay."

"The hay." The dip in Enoch's tone suggested he wasn't convinced.

James met his brother's skeptical gaze. "We need to hire men from town. Extra hands to help bring in the rest of this area and the last two fields before the first snow hits." He eyed the gloomy sky. "A storm could come this week, and we can't lose all that hay."

"Can't spare anyone to ride to town." Enoch took another bite of his sandwich. "Better we buckle down and get it done."

"And the expense—" Robert piped up. "Especially with Rose's wages now added to the books."

"The expense of losing cattle to starvation will be a sight worse than paying a few men for a week's work." James pushed to his feet, brushing crumbs from his hands. The restless energy that had plagued him all morning demanded movement.

He couldn't help a glare at Robert. "Besides, I would've thought you'd be glad for Rose to be here, what with the way you two were mooning at each other this morning."

Robert's sandwich paused halfway to his mouth, and Thomas's brows shot up. Even Enoch turned to stare at him with those piercing blue eyes that saw straight through to a man's soul.

"James." Enoch's tone carried a warning.

But the damage was done. Robert set down his sandwich, his expression thoughtful rather than defensive. "Rose was being polite, nothing more. She's finding her footing here."

"Right." James kicked at a clump of grass, hating himself for the childish display. "Of course she was."

But Robert didn't leave it alone. "She's wary, James. Can't you see that? Whatever happened to her in Virginia City, it's left her gun-shy."

Thomas cleared his throat. "Maybe we should—"

"Enough." Enoch pushed to his feet, brushing off his hands. "James, if you think we need extra hands, ride to town and hire them. Work with them on the two smaller pastures—we should finish this one by the time you're done with those."

James nodded. This would give him something solid to focus on besides his own foolishness. "I'll leave now."

"Good." Enoch's gaze lingered on him with something that might have been sympathy. "Enjoy the ride to town. Clear your head."

As his brothers grabbed their tools for another load, James strode to his horse. It only took a minute to strap on his saddle and bridle, then mount up.

Leaving his brothers behind and setting out on his own felt strange, especially when there was work to be done. But he'd be in charge of the ranch when Enoch and Mandie left for England next year—best he start getting used to making decisions and handling responsibilities on his own.

The gelding's hooves found their rhythm on the familiar trail. He may as well stop at the house and check on the women before riding on to town.

He tried to focus on practical matters as his horse picked its way down the mountainside. How many men could he reasonably hire? Three, maybe four if he could find them. The work would go faster with extra hands, but they'd need to move quickly. Every day they delayed brought winter closer.

Yet his thoughts kept circling back to breakfast, to the careful way Rose had answered their questions about Virginia City. She'd performed there, she'd said. Singing. The word carried weight he couldn't quite decipher. Something that made her shoulders tense and her voice grow distant.

The worst part was Robert's observation: *She's wary, James. Can't you see that?*

Of course he could see it. The way she held herself so carefully, the practiced quality of her smiles, the way she seemed to weigh each word before speaking it. Something had happened to her in Virginia City, something that taught her not to trust.

At the house, the yard showed no sign of the women. When he pushed open the front door, the faint rhythm of their voices drifted from the kitchen. Rose's musical tones blended with Mrs. Wang's brisk chatter and Mandie's gentler interjections.

The sounds drew him like a moth to flame, and he approached the kitchen doorway.

Rose stood at the long wooden counter, her sleeves rolled up to her elbows, flour dusting her apron and blue dress. She was kneading dough at the counter, while Mrs. Wang cut something into a pot at the cookstove, and Mandie sat at the table peeling potatoes. The sight of Rose in the familiar kitchen—her auburn hair tied back in a braid, sunlight streaming through the window to illuminate her profile—made his chest tighten.

Mandie looked up from her potatoes, a smile lighting her face when she spotted him. "James! We weren't expecting you back so soon."

Three pairs of eyes fixed on him, but it was Rose who held his attention. She'd gone still, her hands frozen in the dough, wariness creeping back into her expression like a shadow across sunlit ground. What was it about him that brought that look on every time?

He did his best not to let the frustration slip into his voice. "Just stopping to see if you ladies need anything from town. I'm riding in to hire men to help with the haying."

Mrs. Wang wiped her hands on her apron and bustled toward the pantry. "I make a list for you." She emerged with a scrap of paper and began writing in her precise script. "Salt, more flour, and wicks for the lanterns. Oh, and see if Mr. Henderson has any of those good apples left—the ones that keep well through winter."

Rose's hands continued through the dough, and she kept her gaze honed on her work. Her focus narrowed to the bread as if nothing else existed in the room.

Mandie's voice came in her usual gentle tone. "Rose, would you like James to send a telegram for you? To let anyone know you've arrived safely?"

The kneading stopped. Rose's hands pressed hard into the dough, knuckles whitening. For a moment, something flashed across her features—a quick, raw flicker of fear or pain, sharp enough to make him want to go to her. He had to hold himself back.

"No." The answer came almost on a gasp. "No, thank you. There's no one who needs to know."

The quiet that followed hung thick, as if a storm pressed against the windows. Mrs. Wang cleared her throat and refocused on her writing, but James caught the look she shared with Mandie—a glance that spoke of worry, of questions left unasked.

Rose bent to her work again, kneading the dough with a force that seemed to battle whatever Mandie's simple question had raised in her.

*No one who needs to know.* What kind of life had she left behind in Virginia City, that she had no one—not a soul—to wonder where she'd gone?

He kept his tone light. "Well, the offer stands, if you change your mind."

She nodded without looking up, her movements still carrying that edge of barely controlled tension.

Mrs. Wang pressed the list into his hand. "You be careful on the road. Weather looks ready to turn."

"I will." He pocketed the paper, but couldn't help a glance back at Rose's bent head, the rigid set of her shoulders. The urge to say something—anything—that might ease whatever burden she carried pressed against his ribs like a physical ache.

Instead, he touched the brim of his hat. "Ladies."

The kitchen door closed behind him with a soft click, but Rose's strained expression followed him to his horse and down the trail.

# CHAPTER 7

The scents of sawdust, leather, and vinegar from the pickle barrel drifted through the mercantile as James pushed open the door.

"Afternoon, James." Tom Holbrook glanced up from behind the counter, where he sorted a stack of papers. "What brings you to town?"

James hesitated, gaze shifting to the neat rows of dry goods and tools lining the shelves. "Need to hire some men for the haying. Winter's coming early this year. You know of anyone looking for work? Good, honest men who can swing a scythe?"

"Might be a few down at Nelson's place." Holbrook scratched at his graying beard. "Though most of the able-bodied men are already spoken for, what with the sawmill so busy these days."

James nodded and let his attention wander to the bulletin board near the front window. Notices for cattle sales, animals wanted, odd jobs. The usual.

But right in the center, posted higher and newer than the rest, a single sheet of paper caught his eye. He moved closer, and the bold heading made his blood run cold.

*MISSING PERSON - REWARD OFFERED*

*Rose Prescott, age 19, auburn hair, green eyes, middling height. Last seen Virginia City, Montana Territory. May be traveling under another name. Family worried for her safety. If seen, contact Vincent Dunhill, Virginia City. $50 reward for information leading to her safe return.*

The words blurred before James's eyes as ice flooded his veins. Rose Prescott. His Rose. The woman kneading bread in his kitchen just hours before. This Vincent Dunhill...who was he?

"Something wrong, James?" Holbrook's voice seemed to drift from very far away.

He forced his expression to remain neutral, though his heart hammered against his ribs. "This notice—when did it come in?"

Holbrook glanced over, squinting at the paper. "Yesterday morning, I think. Came through on the telegraph. Mrs. Holbrook posted it." He shrugged. "Don't recognize the name myself, but you never know who might pass through."

Yesterday morning. That was when Rose arrived in Butte on the stage. She'd left Virginia City the day before.

*Fled* Virginia City? Was she in danger from this man?

James's throat constricted as he studied the notice again. *Family worried for her safety.* The words seemed innocent enough, but something about them sat wrong in his gut. If Rose had family in Virginia City who cared about her well-being, why had she told Mandie there was no one who needed to know she'd arrived safely?

"This Vincent Dunhill." He worked for a casual tone. "He say anything else about the girl? Why she might have left?"

Holbrook shook his head. "Just what's written there. Though I got to say, fifty dollars is a mighty generous reward for a missing person notice. Makes a man wonder what the story really is."

Fifty dollars. James's jaw tightened. That was more money than most folks in these parts saw in six months. The kind of reward that suggested either genuine desperation...or something darker.

Mrs. Holbrook emerged from the back room, her arms full of bolts of fabric. "Oh, hello, James. Tom, did you tell him about that poor missing girl?" She set down the cloth and smoothed her graying hair.

James turned and gave a nod of greeting. "Mrs. Holbrook."

"Such a sad thing." She shook her head. "Though I have to wonder what would make a young woman run off like that, leaving her family to worry. The message came through so urgent-like, with instructions to post it in every town from here to the Canadian border."

Every town. James's stomach dropped. If this Vincent Dunhill was casting such a wide net, he wasn't planning to give up easily.

"Did the telegram say anything about why she might have left?"

Mrs. Holbrook shook her head. "Nothing else in the message itself. But you know how these things go—a young woman of that age, probably got her head turned by some smooth-talking fellow promising her the moon." She tsked. "Mark my words, she'll come crawling back home soon enough, once she realizes what the world's really like."

James's jaw clenched at the assumption, but he forced himself to nod as though he agreed. The image of Rose's careful wariness, the way she'd paled when Mandie asked about sending word of her safe arrival, painted a very different picture than Mrs. Holbrook's speculation.

How had he let so many years pass without going after her?

If only he'd traveled to Virginia City when he first learned her whereabouts. He could have seen for himself her situation.

"Well." He stepped back from the notice. "I hope she stays safe, wherever she is."

"Fifty dollars though," Tom mused, returning to his paperwork. "That's serious money. This Dunhill fellow must be mighty worried about her."

Or mighty determined to get her back. The thought twisted his insides.

He pulled Mrs. Wang's memo from his pocket, his hands steadier than he felt. "I'll need these supplies when I'm done hiring men."

As Tom perused the list, James left the mercantile and headed to Nelson's place with leaden feet, the missing person notice burning in his memory like a brand.

The saloon squatted partway down Walnut Springs' main street, its weathered boards dark from years of mountain storms. Even in the afternoon, men's voices and the clink of glasses drifted through the door propped open to allow in fresh air.

James stepped inside, squinting as his eyes adjusted to the dim interior. The familiar stench of whiskey and tobacco smoke hit him, along with the sour tang of men who worked hard and bathed infrequently. A handful of patrons hunched over drinks at the bar, while others clustered around tables in the back.

"James Balfour!" Nelson himself looked up from polishing glasses behind the bar, his Scottish accent still thick after twenty years in Montana Territory. "What brings you to me establishment in broad daylight?"

"Looking for men to hire for a few days." James approached the counter. "Finishing up the haying. Good wages for anyone willing to work hard."

Nelson's weathered face creased into a grin. "Ah, you've

come to the right place then." He raised his voice. "You lads hear that? The Balfour ranch is hiring!"

Three men at a corner table looked up with interest. James recognized two of them—Pete Clawson and his younger brother Jake, both decent workers when sober. The third was a stranger, lean and grizzled with the look of a man who'd seen hard miles.

James walked over to their table. "Afternoon, gentlemen. I need three, maybe four good men for haying work. Meals included, you're welcome to sleep in our barn, and I'll pay a bonus if we beat the weather."

Pete Clawson straightened in his chair, interest flicking in his features. "How much we talking, James?"

"Dollar fifty a day, plus the bonus." It was generous wages, but James needed men who'd work without complaint from dawn to dusk. "If you're willing to come tonight, we'll start tomorrow morning."

"Count me in." Pete glanced at his brother, who nodded eagerly. "Jake's good with a scythe, and we both know the work."

The stranger at their table leaned forward, studying James with sharp eyes. "Name's Bill Carter. I can handle a scythe well enough. Where's your place at?"

As the conversation wound on, he couldn't keep Rose from crowding his thoughts. He needed to get back to the ranch, sit down with her, learn what her life had truly been in Virginia City—and what they were up against now.

Whatever she'd run from, he'd see to it she was safe. No matter what.

# CHAPTER 8

Rose sat between James's empty chair and Robert at the long oak table, listening to the easy flow of dinner conversation around her while darkness pressed against the windows.

The evening had settled around the ranch house like a familiar quilt, and she'd found herself surprisingly at peace during the long afternoon spent learning Mrs. Wang's—Bea's—methods for managing the household. The older woman had insisted Rose call her by her given name like Mandie did, though it appeared the men still addressed her with the formal respect of Mrs. Wang. There was something comforting about that small intimacy, as though she'd been granted entry into an inner circle she'd never expected to find again. What would she do if it were all taken away again?

"The weather's holding better than I expected," Robert was saying as he passed the bowl of roasted potatoes. "If we can get another few days like this one, we might actually beat the snow."

Enoch glanced at the window, though he could surely see nothing with the darkness outside. "James should have been back by now. Hope he didn't run into trouble finding men willing to come up here." The way he said it made Rose's stomach tighten. She set her fork down.

Mandie offered a gentle, "I'm sure he's fine." But her hand drifted to rest protectively over her belly. "Maybe he stayed in town to have supper with the men he hired. It would make sense to talk over the work while they ate."

Hoofbeats sounded in the yard, drawing all their eyes to the window. Thomas pushed back from the table and moved to look out. "That's James. Looks like he's got someone with him. Three someones, actually." Thomas let the curtain fall back into place. "Must have found his workers."

Rose's hands tightened in her lap as the sound of boots on the front porch echoed through the house. Voices carried from outside—James's familiar tone mixed with rougher accents she didn't recognize.

Her pulse quickened, though she couldn't say why. Perhaps it was simply the thought of strangers in this place that had begun to feel like sanctuary.

The voices faded, and the brothers went back to eating.

As though he could sense her confusion, Robert added, "They'll settle the horses before coming in."

She nodded and picked up her fork, though she couldn't bring herself to put a bite in her mouth. What if one of these men had seen her before? What if one of them mentioned her presence here to Vincent? The chances surely weren't likely. She shouldn't worry. Right?

The front door opened, and James's footsteps echoed through the front room.

"Sorry I'm late." He appeared in the doorway. His hair was windblown, his shirt dusty from the road, but his eyes immediately sought Rose's face across the table. Something flickered in his expression—relief, perhaps. At finding her still there? "The men are getting settled in the barn."

Enoch gestured to the empty chair. "We saved you a plate. Who'd you find?"

"Three good ones, I think. Pete and Jake Clawson—you remember them—and a fellow named Bill Carter." James moved to his chair, but his gaze kept returning to Rose with an intensity that made her stomach twist.

"They'll be in to eat in a few minutes." James sank back in his seat. Something in his voice carried an edge she couldn't quite place—tension beneath the casual words. "Mrs. Wang, I hope there's enough food. They've had a long ride."

"Always enough food in this house." Bea rose from her chair and marched into the kitchen. "I get more plates ready."

Rose started to stand as well. "Let me help—"

"No, no. You sit. Eat." Mrs. Wang waved her down, but Rose had already pushed back from the table. The familiar work would give her something to focus on besides the knot of anxiety forming in her chest.

In the kitchen, she helped Mrs. Wang arrange plates while trying to shake the feeling that something had shifted. The way James had looked at her when he'd walked in—not with his usual warmth, but with something that felt almost like worry.

The sound of boots on the porch interrupted her thoughts, followed by voices as the hired men entered the house. She smoothed her skirt and followed Mrs. Wang back into the dining room, carrying the extra plates.

Three men stood by the doorway, hats in hand, the dust of travel still on their clothes. Two of them she could see were brothers—similar build and coloring, though one was younger. The third fellow looked older, lean and weathered, with sharp eyes that took in everything at once.

"Good evening, gentlemen." Enoch rose from his chair. "Welcome to the Balfour ranch."

As the men greeted each other, she placed the plates she

carried on the table, then slipped back into the kitchen. The less time she spent around them the better.

But as she reached for more mugs from the cupboard, James appeared in the kitchen doorway.

"Rose." His voice came quiet, careful. "Could I speak with you a minute?"

Her hands stilled on the cups. The gravity in his tone tightened her chest. "Of course."

Mrs. Wang looked up from ladling potatoes into the bowl, her dark eyes moving between them. "You two go. I finish here."

Rose followed James back through the dining room, then toward the front door. With every step, her insides twisted tighter.

Once outside, he let out a breath. "It'll be quieter here."

More private too. With any other man, she might be worried for her safety or virtue, but this was James. And even if she didn't already know deep inside what a good man he was, she'd spent the entire wagon ride from Butte alone with him, and he'd proved himself a gentleman. Besides, the tense line of his shoulders said he had bad news.

About her, apparently.

James led her to the wooden porch chairs, but he didn't sit, so she didn't either. The evening air carried the sharp bite of coming winter, and Rose wrapped her arms around herself, as much for comfort as warmth.

"Rose." He stopped, running a hand through his hair. In the lamplight spilling from the windows, the conflict in his face showed plain—the way his jaw worked as though searching for the right words.

Her stomach dropped even further. "What is it?"

"There was a notice posted in town today. At Holbrook's mercantile." His green eyes found hers. "A missing person notice. For you."

The world tilted beneath her feet. She gripped the porch

railing, her knuckles white against the weathered wood. "What did it say?"

James's expression grew grim. "Fifty-dollar reward. Posted by Vincent Dunhill in Virginia City." He watched her face carefully. "Says your family is worried for your safety."

Her head went light, and the world swayed a little.

Vincent. Of course he would come after her—she was his investment, his prized songbird. Twenty years of her life signed away on a contract, and he wouldn't let her slip away so easily.

"Rose?" James stepped closer, his hand hovering near her elbow as though he feared she might collapse. "Who is Vincent Dunhill?"

She couldn't speak past the constriction in her throat. He was the man who owned her voice, her time, her very existence until she was thirty-five years old. The man who'd been so generous when Mama lay dying, so understanding about the medical bills and funeral expenses. All she'd had to do was sign her name.

"He's not family," she finally whispered. "He's..."

She couldn't breathe. The mountain air that had felt so clean and fresh all day now seemed thin, insufficient.

Vincent had found her trail already. Of course he had—he had connections everywhere, men who owed him favors. She'd been foolish to think she could simply disappear.

"I have to leave." The words tumbled out before she could stop them. "I have to leave tonight."

"No." James's hand covered hers on the railing, warm and steady. Too solid. "Rose, whatever this is, whatever you're running from, you don't have to leave. My family—we'll protect you. But we have to understand what we're up against."

The knot in her middle twisted tighter at his words. Protect her? How could they protect her from a legal contract signed by her own hand? How could they understand what they were facing when she could barely bring herself to speak it?

"You don't understand." Her voice came out thin. "Vincent isn't just some man looking for a missing girl. He..." She swallowed hard, forcing the words past the shame that rose in her throat like bile. "Mama married him after we left here, then he managed our singing performances. He...required us to sing. When Mama was dying, the doctors, the medicines—it all cost so much money. Vincent paid for everything. The funeral too."

James waited, his hand still covering hers, impossibly still.

"In return, I signed a contract." The admission felt like tearing something vital from her chest. "Twenty years of performances. I owe him until I'm thirty-five years old." She looked up at James then, seeing her own horror reflected in his eyes. "He owns me, Jamie. Legally owns me."

The silence that followed was deafening. James's hand tightened on hers, and his jaw clenched. Something fierce and protective flashed across his features.

"A twenty-year contract?" His voice was barely controlled. "Rose, you were fifteen when your mother died. That's—" He stopped himself, but she could see the word he didn't say written in the hard line of his mouth. Horrible. She'd sold herself, and she was irretrievably horribly dirty.

"I was desperate. Mama was suffering, and the doctors said they could help her, but it cost so much." Even now, the awful weight of it pressed down over her. Smothering.

"Rose." James's voice came out rough, laced with a barely contained fury. "That's not a contract—that's slavery."

She flinched at the word. How it felt so right and yet... "It's legal," she said flatly. "Vincent made sure of that. And now he's looking for me." She turned away from him and stared out into the darkness. "He's not going to let me walk away. He has too much invested in me, and he's not a man who accepts losing what he considers his property. He has connections everywhere. Men who owe him favors, who'll do what he asks without question."

"Then we'll make sure he doesn't find you." James's voice carried a quiet determination that called to her heart. "Rose, listen to me. Whatever papers you signed, they can't be binding. You were a child, desperate and grieving. No court would uphold such a thing."

Rose shook her head, desperation clawing at her throat. "You don't understand. He has money, influence. He could bring the law down on all of you for harboring me. I won't let that happen."

"The law?" James straightened, his voice dropping to an urgent whisper. "Rose, it's not right, and no judge will allow it."

"You think Vincent cares about what's right?" The words came out too loud. Too high-pitched. "He cares about what's profitable. And I'm profitable, James. Very profitable." She wrapped her arms tighter around herself, shield against hope. "He'll find me. He'll make sure everyone believes he's right."

The sound of laughter drifted from the dining room, warm and oblivious to the nightmare unfolding here on the porch. The easy comfort of family life she'd tasted for barely a day was now already slipping away.

"I shouldn't have come here to begin with. I'll go pack my things." She turned toward the door.

"No." James's hand closed around her wrist. "Rose, you're not going anywhere. Not tonight, not until we figure this out together. And by the way, the two-week trial we agreed to doesn't count anymore. I won't let you leave if you'll be in danger. We'll protect you, figure this out together. But you're not going anywhere until it's safe."

The warmth of his touch pulled at the deepest parts of her, and she couldn't stop herself from looking up into his eyes—that familiar green gaze that had once been her anchor in a world that felt too big and frightening outside of the haven of this ranch.

But she wasn't a child anymore, and the world had proven

itself far more dangerous than either of them had imagined all those years ago.

"You don't understand what you're asking." She forced strength into her voice. "If Vincent finds me here, if he brings the authorities—"

"Then we'll deal with it." His thumb brushed across her knuckles, the gesture so gentle it nearly tore down the rest of her determination. "Rose, you're not alone anymore. You have family here. People who care about what happens to you."

Family. The word stirred something deep in her chest that had died so long ago. She'd forgotten what it felt like to have someone stand between her and the world's cruelties, to have someone willing to fight for her simply because she mattered to them.

"You said Vincent has connections everywhere. Men who do his bidding." James spoke with a power that vibrated through her. "But he doesn't have connections here. Not in these mountains. This ranch is five miles from the nearest neighbor, and every man in Walnut Springs has known my family for nearly twenty years. They won't betray us to some stranger from Virginia City, no matter how much money he waves around."

"You can't know that—"

"I can." The nob at his throat worked. "And I can promise you that everyone on this ranch will protect you with our lives. Besides." His voice gentled. "Winter's coming. Even if Vincent does narrow down his search, the mountain passes will be snowed in within weeks. No one's going to be traveling these roads until spring. By then, we can have the details worked out to make that contract null and void. You won't have to worry about Vincent another minute."

She took in a breath, and for the first time in years, the air felt laced with something like hope. Could that really be possible?

The urge to tell him more pressed through her, and she

spoke before her own fears forced her to stop. "I used to pray. When Vincent first took us to Virginia City. I prayed every day for someone to find us. For God to rescue us." She looked down at her hands. "But no one ever came. After a while, I stopped praying. It seemed...pointless."

James was quiet for a long moment. And when he spoke, his voice came rough. "I prayed for you too. Every night after you disappeared. I asked God to keep you safe, to bring you home somehow." His mouth formed a gentle curve. "I didn't know if those prayers reached heaven. But Rose—you're here now. You survived. Maybe God was answering all along, just not in the way either of us expected."

She wanted to believe that. Wanted to believe her suffering had meant something, that God hadn't abandoned her in Virginia City. "But if God was protecting me," she whispered, "why did it take so long?"

"I don't know." He drew a slow breath. "I don't have answers, Rose. But I know God can redeem even the years that were stolen. I have to believe that, or missing you all this time would have drowned me."

The silence that settled between them felt different now—not empty, but full of something fragile. She let herself lean into it. Maybe James was right. Maybe God hadn't abandoned her after all.

His hand found hers in the darkness, his calloused fingers warm against her cold ones. "We'll figure this out together," he said quietly. "The contract, Vincent—all of it. Robert has a good head for legal details. We can get him started on it tonight. If you're up for that."

She stared up at him, searching his face in the lamplight for any sign that this was too good to be true. But his expression held only steady determination and something deeper—a fierce protectiveness that made her chest ache. Maybe if Vincent never found her, she would never have to tell him the rest. Maybe she could simply be part of the family like Bea.

"You really think Robert could help?" Her voice came out small, tentative.

"I know he can. He's been reading law books since he was twelve." He gave her hand a squeeze. "And even if there are legal complications, Rose—you're not going back to that life. Whatever it takes."

A shiver ran through her that had nothing to do with the evening chill. The absolute certainty in his voice stirred something she'd thought Vincent had killed years ago—the belief that someone might actually fight for her.

Letting out the breath of fear, she gave a nod. "All right. If you're sure you want to try."

# CHAPTER 9

The sound of the three hired men leaving the house to settle into the barn for the night had barely faded when James cleared his throat and looked around the dining room table. "Before we all turn in, I think we need to have a family meeting."

Mrs. Wang stood and began gathering the empty plates from dinner. "I clean up the kitchen—"

"Actually." He raised a hand to halt her. "We'd like you to take part, if you would. This concerns Rose, and she's going to need all of us."

The older woman paused, a stack of plates balanced in her weathered hands, and looked between James and Rose with those sharp eyes. Whatever she saw made her set the dishes back down with a soft clink.

"Of course." She settled back into her chair, folding her hands in her lap with her usual quiet dignity. "Rose is family."

His sentiment exactly.

Enoch leaned back in his chair, his piercing gaze moving between James and Rose. "What kind of trouble are we talking about?"

James looked at Rose, waiting for her permission. They'd talked about this on the porch—the need to tell everyone at least the basic details. This way, they could best protect her, and also, they could work together to break Vincent's control over her permanently.

She'd been hesitant, though she'd agreed. Now, she gave a barely perceptible nod, but her shoulders had gone rigid again.

He turned back to the others, choosing his words with care. "Rose is being pursued by a man named Vincent Dunhill from Virginia City. He's posted missing person notices offering a fifty-dollar reward for information about her whereabouts."

Thomas whistled low. "Fifty dollars? That's serious money."

Robert studied her. "What's his connection to you, Rose?"

Rose's hands clenched in her lap, her knuckles white against the blue fabric of her skirt.

"He was my stepfather," she said finally, her voice almost too soft to hear. "Mama married him after we left here. When she became ill, he paid for everything. Even…" She swallowed hard, the delicate lines of her throat working against whatever words were trying to escape. "The funeral expenses."

Mrs. Wang made a soft sound of sympathy, her face creasing with concern.

"In return." Rose's voice gained a little strength. "I signed a contract. Twenty years of performances. Until I'm thirty-five."

This was too painful, making her answer the questions. He could relay the basic information his family needed. Part of him wanted to close his hand over her clenched ones, anything to help settle her. To let her know she was safe here. But she looked like even that touch might crack her.

At least he could take over the weight of the explanation. "Vincent has used the contract to control her. To basically keep her prisoner. She sneaked away to come to us, but now he's looking for her. Rose said he has a lot of connections, men who will help accomplish what he wants, even if it's not quite lawful." He met each of his brothers' gazes in turn. "We'll need to protect her, and we'll need to figure out how to break that contract for good."

The silence that followed felt heavy, charged with the kind of tension that preceded mountain storms. Thomas's easy smile had faded. Mandie's hand covered her belly. Enoch's jaw tightened with controlled anger.

Robert leaned forward, his lawyer's mind already working. "A twenty-year contract signed by a fifteen-year-old?" His voice carried a sharp edge. "Rose, do you have a copy of this document?"

She shook her head. "Vincent kept all the papers in his office. He said it was safer that way."

"Of course he did." Robert's tone turned grim. "Rose, I need you to understand something. A contract signed by a minor under duress—especially one involving twenty years of labor— that's not just unenforceable, no legitimate court would uphold such a thing."

Hope flickered in Rose's green eyes, fragile as candlelight in a draft. But it was quickly shadowed by fear. "Vincent has friends in the territorial government. Judges, lawyers, men who owe him favors. He's made that very clear over the years. He says the law will always side with him."

Enoch leaned forward, bracing his elbows on the table. "He's not the only one with connections. Our father is the Duke of Clarence, distant cousin of Queen Victoria. I know that's in England and this is America, but we still have a long list of people in the Montana Territory and beyond who would be more than willing to listen to the facts of the case, especially when their attention is requested by the Duke of Clarence or one of his sons."

Rose straightened, and something that looked almost like hope crossed her features. "You're titled aristocracy." She spoke as though testing the words. "I'd forgotten."

"Most people out here have." Enoch's smile held a hint of irony. "But the connections remain. Vincent Dunhill may have territorial judges in his pocket, but he doesn't have access to federal courts. Or to the kind of legal minds we can call on."

So many emotions played across Rose's face—hope warring with years of learned caution. Her hands had unclenched in her lap, though she still held herself with that brittle tension he'd come to recognize as her armor against the world.

"Good." Robert's expression grew more confident, the analytical mind James had always admired clearly working through the legal implications. "From what you've described, Rose, this contract should be easily proven invalid. We just need a copy of it."

Rose's face went ashen, and his gut clenched. That fragile hope that had been building in her eyes flickered and died like a candle in a sudden wind.

"I don't have a copy." Her voice turned quiet again. "Vincent insisted on keeping my copy with all the other papers associated with my work. He said they belonged in 'our' office at Murphy's —that's the saloon where I performed. He said it was more professional that way, more secure."

The silence that followed felt suffocating. Rose shrank back into herself, her shoulders curving inward as though she were trying to disappear entirely. Every line of her body spoke of defeat, a woman who'd allowed herself to hope for a moment only to have that hope crushed again.

"Of course he kept them," Thomas muttered. "Can't have his property knowing exactly what rights she might have."

Robert pinched his lips together as he thought. "We'll see what we can do without it then." He looked to Enoch. "Think we should telegraph Father for a list of solicitors and judges to speak with?"

Enoch nodded. "Someone can ride to town to send it as soon

as we finish the haying." He glanced toward James, almost like he was looking for approval of the plan.

As much as James hated to wait the three or four days that would take, he couldn't deny the desperate need to get the hay in before the snow came. It could mean life or death for their herds through the winter. And hopefully, a few days' delay in their efforts to free Rose wouldn't matter, since she would be safe and protected here on the ranch.

So he gave his brother a small nod, then glanced at Rose to make sure she understood the reason for the delay.

She looked hesitant, as though she didn't quite follow what they were thinking.

He dropped his voice lower, just for her. "If we don't get the hay cut and stored before the first snow, we'll lose it. But the moment that's done, I'll take the telegram to town. You're safe here with us though. Vincent won't be able to find you here."

She searched his gaze, and he let her see his certainty. Even if the man did somehow search out her location, he and his brothers would die before letting her go back to that slavery.

At last, she nodded. "Thank you." She moved her gaze around the table to each person sitting there. "Thank you all."

Mrs. Wang reached across the wooden surface. "You are home now, child. We take care of you."

# CHAPTER 10

*T*he first snowflakes fell like whispered warnings against the kitchen window as Rose placed a cloth over the soaking beans. The men were pushing so hard to get the hay stored before this very event.

From what Enoch said that morning, they still had at least two more days' work after today. Maybe this would only be a few flakes. Not enough to stick.

*For their sakes, God, maybe You could make it hold off.* God hadn't answered her prayers in so many years, but perhaps for the Balfours, He'd listen.

"Rose, child." Mrs. Wang—Bea—appeared at her elbow, drying her hands on her apron. "Mandie's gone up for her nap, poor thing. This baby's wearing her out." She glanced toward the window where the snow continued its gentle assault. "Snow comes when it comes." Her mouth curved into a soft smile. "God sends it, so we take what He sends and make warm food." She winked as if it were the simplest arithmetic.

She could barely fathom faith like that. No bargaining. Just a peace that what God sent would be exactly what they needed. No fear that one misstep might turn His face away.

Bea motioned for her. "Come with me. There's something I want to show you while we have a quiet moment."

Rose followed her through the house and up the wooden stairs, their footsteps muffled by the thick runner. They passed the room where Rose was staying, as well as those of the three younger brothers. At the end of the hallway, Bea opened a narrow door that led to another set of stairs, steeper and more cramped than the main staircase.

"Mind your head." Bea pointed to the low rafters as they climbed into the attic.

The space was dim and dusty, filled with the scents of old wood and dust. Weak light filtered through a small window at the far end, illuminating cobwebs dancing in the drafts. She had to duck a little as she followed Bea, her skirts brushing against wooden crates and cloth-covered furniture.

"Here we are." Bea stopped beside a medium-sized wooden crate, its surface gray with dust. She brushed the top clean with her hand, revealing faded initials carved into the wood: M.P. "This belonged to your mama, child. And to you."

Rose's breath caught in her throat. Margaret Prescott. Her mother's name, before Vincent, before everything had changed.

"These are all the things I found when we cleaned out your room after you and your mama left so sudden-like." Bea rested her hands on the crate's lid. "I kept them here in case you ever came back."

Rose's chest clenched, and she dropped to her knees beside the box. Bea moved aside to allow her access.

She brushed a hand over the carved initials. Eleven years. These things had waited here gathering dust while she'd been trapped in Virginia City.

Her fingers trembled as she lifted the wooden lid.

On top lay a small wooden doll, its painted face faded but still smiling. Rose's throat tightened as she lifted it from the crate. She'd carried this doll everywhere during those early days at the ranch, whispering her secrets during the long nights when this new world felt too big and frightening.

"I—" Her voice caught. "I thought she was gone."

"You called her Emma." Bea's gentle murmur felt like a hug—a mother's hug. "Used to have tea parties with her in the garden behind the kitchen. You'd make the younger boys come join you, as often as you could talk them into it."

She cradled the doll against her chest, the weight of memory settling around her like a familiar shawl.

Emma. She'd forgotten the name, but now it came flooding back with images of summer afternoons spent arranging wildflowers in tiny cups, chattering away to her companions about everything and nothing. Most of the time that companion had been James, but occasionally Robert or Thomas, or even a pretty leaf or rock she found, if the boys were occupied elsewhere.

Beneath the doll lay other treasures—a wooden box filled with colored stones she'd collected from the creek, a book of fairy tales with her name written in careful childish script inside the front cover, and a small blue hair ribbon Mama used to tie in her braids.

But it was the items clearly belonging to her mother that surged tears to her eyes. A pair of white gloves, yellowed now but still soft. A small leather journal with a brass clasp. A glance inside showed its pages filled with her mother's careful handwriting.

Rose lifted the journal. She'd never seen this before—Mama must have hidden it away, keeping her private thoughts safe from prying eyes. The leather was worn smooth, as though it had been handled often.

She traced the brass clasp with her fingertip. The thought of reading her mother's words felt both precious and intrusive, as if she were stepping into a sacred space she'd never truly been invited to enter.

"There's more underneath," Bea prodded. Maybe she realized reading these might be too much for now.

Rose set the journal aside and reached deeper into the crate. Her fingers found fabric. Silk, by the feel of it. She drew out a cream-colored shawl, so fine it was nearly transparent, with delicate blue embroidery along the edges. The threads had tarnished a little with age, but the pattern of tiny roses and leaves, was still clear, worked in what had once been silver.

"Your mama wore that for special occasions." Bea's voice hummed soft with memory. "Lady Balfour gave it to her the Christmas before she died. Said it brought out the color of Margaret's eyes."

Rose held the shawl up to the dim light filtering through the small window. She could almost see her mother in it, could almost remember the way it had floated around her shoulders as she walked. The silk was so delicate it felt like it might dissolve at her touch. Yet it had survived all these years in this dusty attic, waiting.

Mama had said so many kind things about Lady Balfour, what a gracious and giving woman she was.

A memory crept in, one she'd long since forgotten about. Mama had mentioned something else she accidentally left at the Balfour ranch during their sudden departure. A treasure she'd longed for, but didn't dare go back for or even send a letter of inquiry.

Rose glanced at Bea. Would it be all right to ask? Surely so. Bea had been nothing but overwhelmingly kind since Rose returned. "Do you remember a necklace and eardrops my mother also left behind? I believe they were a gift from Lady Balfour too. Rubies, I think."

Bea's face grew thoughtful, her dark eyes distant as she reached back through the years. "Rubies..." She pressed her lips together. "I remember them. Beautiful pieces—a necklace with three teardrop stones and matching earbobs. Lady Balfour gave them to your mama for her birthday that last spring."

Rose's heart quickened, and heat burned at her eyes. They did exist. The memory wasn't some fevered dream from childhood.

"But I haven't seen them since you left, child." Bea's hands smoothed her apron, an act that seemed to be the older woman's way of thinking through a problem. "I cleaned your mama's room myself after you moved away, packed everything I could find. If they'd been there, they would have gone in this crate with the rest."

The disappointment settled in Rose's chest like a stone, though she'd hardly dared hope the jewelry would still be here after all these years. Still, the loss felt fresh, as though she were losing her mother all over again.

Bea tapped her finger against her chin. "I suppose if they were left behind and we didn't find them, they would still be in your old room. The one you're staying in now. Your mama kept her jewelry box on the little table by the window, remember? Sometimes precious things slip behind furniture and get forgotten when we're in a hurry. We can ask the men to move the chest of drawers when they come in tonight so we can do a proper search."

Rose nodded, though she couldn't wait for tonight. She could shift the furniture herself.

After placing her treasures back in the crate, she stood and smiled at Bea. "Thank you. Thank you for keeping it all safe."

The older woman's hand settled on her shoulder. "They were always yours, child. I was just the caretaker until you came home."

Home. That word again, wrapping around her like the silk shawl had wrapped her mother's shoulders all those years ago.

Yet this *wasn't* her home. It couldn't be. Vincent had already proven this place was far too close for any lasting safety or peace. She would stay safe here through the winter, and in spring when the rivers thawed, she might have enough saved for passage east. Surely St. Louis would be far enough from Vincent's clutches.

She could find work there. She could start over completely. Find a respectable job, perhaps as a music teacher for children of wealthy families. Use her voice for something beautiful again, instead of as bait to keep men drinking and gambling away their decency.

She carried the wooden crate back to her room, her arms trembling a little under its weight—though whether from the physical burden or the emotional one, she couldn't say.

Her chamber felt different now, full of possibility. She set the box on the bed and moved to the window where the snow continued its gentle descent. The flakes were larger now, more persistent, though they still didn't stick to the ground below. Her heart clenched for the men working desperately in the fields.

But she had her own task to accomplish.

Finding that necklace and eardrops would give her one more treasure to connect with Mama. And she would have it as an option to sell if she needed more money on her journey. She would never dream of taking anything from the Balfour home, but this…this was her own mother's belongings that had been lost.

She turned to study the heavy oak chest of drawers against the far wall. It was an enormous piece, clearly built to last generations, and she could see why Bea thought it might need the men's strength to move. But Rose had learned to be resourceful during her years in Virginia City. She'd had to be.

She pushed against one corner of the chest, testing its weight. The frame groaned in protest but shifted a little, revealing a sliver of dusty floor behind it. Her pulse quickened.

If something had fallen back there during their hasty departure all those years ago…

Bracing her shoulder against the side of the chest, she pushed harder. The heavy piece scraped across the wooden floor with a sound that made her wince, but it moved another few inches. Dust danced in the afternoon light filtering through the window, and she could see more of the space behind the furniture now.

Nothing metal glinted there.

She pushed harder, her muscles straining against the stubborn furniture. The chest scraped another inch across the floor, leaving grooves in the dust. Still nothing but bare wooden planks and accumulated grime.

She wiped her brow with her sleeve. Perhaps the jewelry had never fallen behind the furniture at all. Perhaps Vincent had somehow gotten his hands on it years ago, through means she didn't want to contemplate. He'd always been resourceful when it came to acquiring things of value.

But she couldn't give up. Not yet.

With a final straining push, she managed to shift the chest far enough to reveal the entire space behind it. Her heart sank as she stared at the empty floor, marked only by the rectangular outline where the furniture had stood for years.

No glint of ruby. No jewelry box that might have slipped into the shadows. Just dust and disappointment.

She sank onto the edge of the bed, her body drooping with exhaustion that had little to do with moving furniture. Of course the necklace wasn't there. Nothing in her life had ever been that simple, that easy. She'd been foolish to hope that something so valuable would simply be waiting for her after all these years. Vincent had probably claimed it long ago, adding it to his collection of things that had once belonged to her mother.

She glanced at the wooden crate beside her, its contents now feeling even more precious. At least she had these memories, these tangible pieces of the life she'd shared with Mama before everything changed. The wooden doll gazed up at her with painted eyes that seemed to hold all the innocence she'd lost.

She may not be innocent anymore, but at least she had a plan. She'd escaped from Vincent, and by this time next year, she'd be in St. Louis.

Living her new life. A life she would finally have control over.

# CHAPTER 11

The knot in James's stomach tightened as he watched Mrs. Holbrook's fingers tap against the telegraph key, each metallic click echoing through the mercantile like a hammer against his nerves.

They'd finally finished bringing in the hay—every piece now safely stored in their sheds, ready to see the cattle through whatever winter threw at them. Pete, Jake, and Bill Carter had earned every cent of their wages, working from dawn to dusk without complaint. The relief should be overwhelming.

Instead, all he could think about was Rose's face when he'd left that morning, the way she'd watched him saddle his horse with worry flicking in those green eyes.

"There." Mrs. Holbrook finally lifted her hands from the device. "Your message should reach your father within the hour, assuming the lines are clear all the way."

"Thank you." He'd asked Father to reply by tomorrow morning, if possible. He wasn't certain how quickly his father could compile the list of legal contacts they needed though.

Mrs. Holbrook flashed a smile that seemed too bright for the gravity of what he'd just sent. "I must say, it's exciting to think of all those important men your father knows. Judges and solic-itors—what grand connections the Balfours have."

The praise sat uncomfortable in his gut. The Holbrooks had started the mercantile around the time his family moved to the territory and built the ranch, so they knew of the Balfours' aris-tocratic ties. "We appreciate your discretion, Mrs. Holbrook."

"Of course, of course." She bustled around the counter, straightening papers that didn't need straightening. "I do hope everything works out for whoever needs the help."

They'd kept the telegram vague—a request for contacts among territorial judges and attorneys, men of unquestionable reputation who might assist with a contract dispute. Nothing that would raise questions or draw unwanted attention.

Mrs. Holbrook looked up at him, as though she'd just remembered something. "By the way, I realized something about that missing person notice after you left the other day."

Ice flooded his veins. But he forced his expression to remain casual even as every muscle in his body went tight. "Oh?"

"The woman's surname is Prescott. Isn't that the same name as the lady's maid your mother used to have?"

His chest constricted even more. Of course she would remember. Mrs. Holbrook had made it her business to know every detail about the English family with ties to nobility that had settled in their mountains. And while his mother was alive, she'd insisted their family maintain some semblance of English propriety in the Montana wilderness.

"Your mother was such an elegant lady, always so gracious to everyone. And she was quite fond of Mrs. Prescott. They used to come to town together sometimes, shopping for fabrics and such. Whatever happened to that woman? She left suddenly, didn't she, after your mother passed? And didn't she have a daughter—a little red-haired thing who used to follow you boys around?"

The metallic taste of panic flooded his mouth. He forced

himself to swallow, to keep his expression politely interested rather than horrified. "I was just a boy then. I don't remember all the details. I think her mother remarried and they moved away." His voice sounded steady enough, though his heart hammered against his ribs. "We lost contact with them after that." It wasn't fully a lie. Was it? Just not all the truth.

Mrs. Holbrook nodded. "Such a shame when people drift apart like that. I always wondered what became of them." She paused, her fingers drumming against the counter. "This missing person notice—Rose Prescott, age twenty. That would be about right for the little girl I remember, wouldn't it? She'd be a grown woman now."

The blood roared in his ears. He managed what he hoped passed for a casual shrug. "Could be, I suppose. Prescott's not an uncommon name."

"No, I suppose not." But her eyes held a calculating gleam that made his stomach churn. "Still, what are the chances? A red-haired girl with the last name of Prescott, the same as your mother's maid. Makes you wonder, doesn't it?"

Every instinct screamed at him to get out of there, to end this conversation before Mrs. Holbrook's curiosity led her to conclusions that could destroy Rose's safety. But leaving too abruptly would also fuel her suspicions.

"Well." He forced his tone to remain light. "I hope wherever she is, she's safe. Good day, Mrs. Holbrook."

He touched the brim of his hat and turned to exit, his movements feeling stiff and unnatural. Each step toward the door felt like walking through thick mud, as though the weight of Mrs. Holbrook's suspicions dragged at his boots.

"See you later, Mr. Balfour. Thanks again for the work." Bill Carter tipped his hat to James as he walked by where the man perused the winter coats. He'd forgotten Bill was in here, doing a bit of shopping with the wages he'd earned from the haying.

James forced a friendly expression as he slowed and nodded

to the man. "Thanks again for all your help, Bill. I'm not sure we would have finished that last field in time without you."

A modest smile tipped one side of his mouth. "We got it done though. Glad I could be of service."

James moved on to the door and stepped out into the crisp mountain air, each breath visible in small white puffs. The door closed behind him with a soft chime, but Mrs. Holbrook's curious gaze followed him through the window.

Every fiber of his being wanted to get back to the ranch, to make sure Rose was still safe within those log walls. But he'd planned to spend a night in town to receive his father's return wire before he rode home. He had to follow through with that.

The boarding house sat just down the street, its painted sign creaking in the afternoon wind. Mrs. Patterson would have a room—she always did after the first snow, when the mining crews had headed down to warmer elevations and the loggers left for winter.

The boarding house door opened before he could knock, and Mrs. Patterson's weathered face peered out at him.

"James Balfour. What brings you to town overnight?" She stepped aside to let him enter, her gray hair pinned back in its usual severe bun. "Don't tell me there's trouble at the ranch."

"No trouble." The lie came easier than it should have. "Just waiting for a telegram from my father. Thought I'd stay the night rather than ride back and forth."

"Of course, dear. I've got a nice room on the second floor, overlooks the street." She bustled toward the desk in the corner to pick up the key. "Supper's at six if you'd like to join us. Nothing fancy, but it's hot and filling."

James followed her up the creaking stairs, his mind still churning over Mrs. Holbrook's questions. The woman had always been curious about other people's business, but this felt different. More pointed. The way she'd connected the dots between the missing person notice and Rose's childhood at the ranch made his chest tight with dread.

"Here we are." Mrs. Patterson unlocked a door halfway down the hall and pushed it open. "Clean blankets, fresh water in the pitcher. Will this suit you?"

"It's perfect. Thank you."

The room was small but tidy, with a narrow bed, a washstand, and a single window that looked out onto the main street. Mrs. Patterson handed him the key and stepped back.

After she left, he sank onto the edge of the bed and dropped his head into his hands. The silence of the room felt oppressive after the constant worry that had plagued him since leaving the ranch that morning.

Mrs. Holbrook's words echoed in his mind: *A red-haired girl with the last name of Prescott, the same as your mother's maid. Makes you wonder, doesn't it?*

He should have anticipated this. Should have realized that the older residents of Walnut Springs would remember Rose's mother, would make the connection between the missing person notice and the Prescotts who had once lived at the Balfour ranch.

At least people thought the Prescotts had long ago left the area. No matter what, he had to make sure Rose never came to town.

# CHAPTER 12

The ink had faded to brown on the yellowed pages, but each word still held the weight of her mother's voice. Rose traced her finger along Mama's careful script, each letter a lifeline to a woman who felt increasingly distant with every passing day.

*March 15th - Rose and Master James have become such good friends, especially since we came to the American territories with the Balfours. It warms my heart to see them so happy, though I know theirs can never be more than friendship. He sits at tea with her and her dolly, and she goes fishing with him, catching just as many or more than the lad does.*

Rose closed her eyes, letting herself linger in the memories—the warm afternoons by the creek, James's patient hands showing her how to bait the hook, the way he'd never once suggested fishing wasn't proper for a girl. She could almost smell the pine sap and hear the gentle murmur of water over stones.

The silence of the house wrapped around her like a familiar

quilt as she read through the journal for the third time. Downstairs, the soft sounds of a Saturday afternoon winding toward evening—the gentle tick of the mantel clock, the occasional creak of settling timber.

Bea and Mandie had both gone to rest after finishing preparations for supper, and even the men were taking a break after the long hard days of haying. Enoch had gone out to the barn, Robert to the study to answer correspondence, and Thomas had claimed the great room with whatever novel captured his attention this week.

She turned the page in the journal, hungry for more glimpses of that golden time.

*April 2nd - Rose has been helping Mrs. Wang in the kitchen again today. The dear woman is so patient with her, teaching her to knead bread and roll pastry. Rose takes such pride in her work, and I confess it brings me joy to see her learning skills that will serve her well. Though I pray she will never need to earn her living by them.*

The irony of those last words cut deep. If only Mama could see her now—twenty years old and finally free of Vincent's control. She was more than grateful to be back on the ranch, working once again with Mrs. Wang in the kitchen.

Another entry, dated two weeks later:

*Rose asked me today why we cannot stay here forever. Such a difficult question from one so young. How can I explain that our place in this household depends entirely on the Balfours' continued goodwill? That we are servants, no matter how kindly we are treated? She sees only the love they show her, the way young Master James includes her in everything. She does not understand that we live here by their grace alone, and grace can be withdrawn.*

The words stung, even after all these years. Had Mama really believed they were only tolerated? She'd felt so completely part of the family, racing through the house with Thomas, helping Mrs. Wang in the kitchen, sitting by the fire while Enoch read aloud from adventure books. Had it all been an illusion?

*May 3rd – I met a gentleman in town today, Mr. Vincent Dunhill. He was most courteous, holding the door at the mercantile and carrying my parcels to the wagon. He has recently arrived from back east and spoke of business opportunities in Virginia City. Such refined manners and conversation—quite unlike the rough miners we typically encounter.*

Rose's stomach clenched. So this was how it had started. A chance meeting. Polite gestures. The same charm Vincent had wielded like a weapon for as long as she'd known him.

*May 17th - Mr. Dunhill called at the ranch today with flowers for Lady Balfour and myself. Such a thoughtful gesture. He stayed for tea and entertained us with stories of his travels. Lady Balfour was polite, but she seemed reserved. Perhaps she is unused to receiving callers in this wilderness. Certainly she's not embarrassed of this magnificent home.*

*May 24th - Vincent (he insists I call him by his Christian name) has been calling twice weekly now. He brings such interesting conversation and has expressed great interest in my singing. He says I have a natural talent that shouldn't be hidden away on a ranch. Lady Balfour spoke to me after his last visit, cautioning me to be careful. She says something about him troubles her, though she couldn't say exactly what. I assured her Vincent is a perfect gentleman.*

Rose's throat tightened. Lady Balfour had seen through him even then. Had tried to warn her mother. But Mama had been too smitten to listen.

*June 1st - Lady Balfour spoke to me again today about Vincent. She was more direct this time, saying she fears he's only interested in what he might gain—that he seems the type to always be looking for easy money or advantage. Her words stung, I confess. Why does she think he isn't visiting simply because he appreciates my company? He has been nothing but kind and attentive. I told her she doesn't know him as well as I do, that beneath his polished exterior is a man of genuine feeling.*

*June 8th - Vincent asked permission to court me properly. My heart soared. But when I mentioned it to Lady Balfour, she became worried. She took my hands and begged me to wait, to take more time before making any commitments. She says there's something not right about a man who appears so suddenly and moves so quickly.*

The entries that followed grew shorter, more distant, as though Mama had stopped confiding fully in her journal—or perhaps had been too busy with Vincent's attentions to write as much.

*June 15th - Lady Balfour grows weaker each day. The doctor says there is nothing more to be done. I see the fear in the boys' eyes, though they try to be brave. Rose has been reading to her ladyship in the afternoons, her sweet voice bringing the only smiles we see anymore. Vincent has been so supportive during this difficult time, bringing medicine he says might help. I pray...*

The entry ended there, the ink trailing off like Mama had been interrupted. She stared at the incomplete sentence, wishing desperately that she could know what prayer had been on her mother's heart in that moment.

And those other words... *Bringing medicine he says might help.*

The words seemed to pulse on the page, innocent on the surface but laden with terrible meaning now that she knew the truth. Had that been when it started? When Vincent had begun poisoning Lady Balfour under the guise of helping?

She flipped through several more pages, most containing brief notes about Lady Balfour's declining health, until she found another entry that brought the burn of tears to her eyes.

*July 10th - Lady Balfour passed peacefully this morning. The boys are devastated, especially young William, who feels the weight of being eldest so keenly. Enoch holds his grief stoically, but James is just the opposite. Rose has not left his side all day, holding his hand while they both weep. Robert and Thomas are so young, I'm not sure they know why they're crying. Only that there is such grief here, it weighs thick in the air.*

*I fear what this means for our future here. Lord Balfour has not yet arrived from England, though he left when we first realized Lady Balfour's illness had begun to worsen. Will he take the boys back with him? Where will that leave Rose and me? I have only ever been a lady's maid, but I no longer have a lady to serve.*

Rose's throat tightened as she remembered that terrible day —the hushed voices, the black crepe draped over mirrors, James's red-rimmed eyes as they sat together on the porch steps. She'd been so focused on comforting him that she hadn't understood the precariousness of her own situation.

She turned the page, desperate for more of her mother's voice, for more understanding of what had driven them away from the only home she'd ever truly known.

*July 25th - Lord Balfour finally arrived today. He is a stern man, though I can see the grief carved into every line of his face. He spoke briefly with me about the household arrangements. I am to remain on to help Mrs. Wang until other plans are made. Rose may continue her lessons with the boys' tutor. Nothing permanent, he made clear, but we are not to be turned out immediately.*

Relief flooded through Rose, even knowing how the story would end. At least there had been those few extra months, that precious time when she'd still believed the ranch would always be her home…that James would always be her best friend.

Voices downstairs pulled her focus from the page, though it took a minute longer for her middle to uncoil from the reminders of how Vincent had charmed his way into controlling Mama. He'd been a viper who concealed his true purpose until Margaret Prescott had committed her life to him before God and man. Then he'd exploited her singing abilities any and every chance he could—including blackmail.

One of the voices downstairs carried the deeper timbre of James, so she set the book aside. Maybe he brought news from Lord Balfour.

She made her way down the stairs, one hand trailing along the banister she'd polished yesterday. The afternoon light streaming through the tall windows had taken on that golden quality that spoke of evening approaching, casting long shadows across the wooden floors.

In the great room, James stood near the fireplace with a paper in his hands. His brothers crowded around, peering at the document.

When she stepped into the room, James's green eyes found hers, and something in his expression made her stomach flutter with nervous anticipation. "Rose. Perfect timing. I have Father's reply."

She moved closer. "What does he say?"

"He's provided a list of names—solicitors and territorial judges who have impeccable reputations and no ties to Virginia City interests." James's voice carried a note of satisfaction that stirred hope in her chest. "Men who could be allies for us."

Robert looked up from the list. "I guess the question is, should we visit them all in person? Or start with letters?"

Enoch frowned. "Letters first, I think. They'll reach the men before we could visit in person, and that way they'll have time to research our family if they wish."

Thomas shifted closer to the paper, squinting at the script. "How many judges does he list?"

"Three territorial judges and four solicitors with experience in contract law." James folded the telegram carefully. "Father says Judge Harrison in Helena has handled several cases involving unconscionable contracts, and he knows the solicitors in Fort Benton and Bannock personally."

Rose's heart hammered against her ribs. These men, these Balfour brothers who had once been her dearest friends, were marshaling resources she couldn't have imagined to help her. The scope of their father's connections, the weight of influence they could bring to bear on her behalf—it felt almost too much to believe.

But would they still help her if they knew what Vincent had done, what her mother had done? Surely they would listen, would understand. James had said she'd been a child.

And she had been, but that didn't always seem to matter. *Like mother, like daughter*, Vincent had said. As if sensing her fears, James squeezed her elbow and smiled.

"It would be helpful to have a copy of the contract though." Robert tapped his finger against his chin. "Even the best legal minds will need to see the actual document to build a proper case."

That familiar knot twisted in her middle. "Vincent keeps all the papers in his office at Murphy's."

Thomas looked up from studying the list. "Where exactly is this office? What part of the building?"

"Behind the main saloon." Down the long hallway she'd had to traverse to reach the stairs to her own chamber.

"Is it locked?" Thomas pressed. "The office, I mean."

She studied him. "He always kept it locked." Surely Thomas wasn't actually planning to sneak in to retrieve the contract.

Silence fell over the room, and something shifted in the air. Thomas glanced at his brothers, then back at her with an expression that seemed almost…calculating.

"Thomas." James's voice carried a warning note that made Rose's skin prickle.

But Thomas ignored his brother, leaning forward with a new intensity. "Rose, tell me more about the layout. How do you get to Vincent's office from the main entrance? And who all has keys?"

That twist in her middle turned a little tighter. "Vincent has the only key I know of." Should she allow Thomas to attempt this madness? It was dangerous, but if he was discovered, would Vincent realize Thomas's connection to her? She forced herself to focus on a thorough answer to his question. "I suppose Murphy might have one too, since it's his building."

"What about windows? Any way to get in from outside?"

"Thomas." This time James's warning carried real steel.

But Rose found herself answering anyway, drawn in by something in Thomas's manner that made it impossible not to go along with him. At least to give him the information he asked for. "The only windows facing the back of the building are on the second floor. No windows on either side of the building. On the front, there's just those at the saloon."

Thomas straightened, and something hardened in his expression—a determination that reminded her of Enoch when he'd made up his mind about something.

"I'll go," Thomas said simply. "I'll get your copy of the contract."

Rose's breath stalled. The casual way he said it, as though he were volunteering to fetch supplies from town rather than break into Vincent's locked office, made her chest clench.

"Absolutely not." James stepped forward, his voice sharp. "Thomas, that's—"

"Necessary." Thomas cut him off with a look that brooked

no argument. "Rose needs that contract to prove what Vincent did to her. We all know it. And I'm the logical choice to go—I'm the only one of us who knows how to get in and out of places quietly. And I can talk my way through anything."

"That's the truth." Robert's mumble did nothing to quell the panic rising in her chest.

She sucked in a breath, then forced herself to push it out slowly. "Vincent isn't just dangerous—he's ruthless. If he catches you, if he finds out where I am..." She couldn't finish the thought. The image of Thomas trapped in that smoky back room, facing Vincent's cold fury, made her feel sick.

But Thomas's expression remained steady, almost gentle. "Vincent doesn't know me from any other miner in the territory. If he did catch me, he'd just think I was a drifter looking for something to steal. He has no reason to connect me to you."

She clenched her skirts as she stared at him. The easy confidence in his voice only made her worry more.

Then his mouth tipped on one side, his eyes taking on that mischievous glint she was becoming familiar with. "Rose, I've been in and out of places I wasn't supposed to be since I could walk. This is just another locked door."

Robert frowned. "It's awfully risky. You could get caught."

Thomas flashed another grin. "You know me, brother. I never get caught. Besides, I can mail the letters to those judges and solicitors while I'm out. Maybe even hand-deliver a couple."

She stared at Thomas, her chest tightening with each word he spoke. The fire popped in the hearth behind him, but the sound seemed muted beneath the roar of her own pulse in her ears. He made it sound so simple, so reasonable—as though Vincent were just another obstacle to overcome rather than the calculating predator who had owned her life for five years.

"Thomas, you don't know him." The words scraped against her throat. "Vincent isn't like other men. He's...he watches everything. Studies people. He has ways of making you tell him things you never meant to say."

The memory of his pale eyes surfaced unbidden—the way he could look at a person and peel back every layer of pretense until nothing remained but naked truth. How many times had she watched him break down a man's defenses with nothing more than patient questions and that terrible, knowing smile?

Thomas's expression gentled, and he took a step closer. "Rose, I understand you're scared. But Vincent's never met me. At least, not since I was a tot. He has no reason to suspect I'm anything more than another drifter looking for easy money. Men like that—they expect petty theft. They don't expect someone with actual skill."

She forced herself to take in a breath. Maybe he was right.

A hand rested on her lower back. Gentle. Reassuring.

James.

The warmth of his palm spread through the fabric of her dress, but it couldn't quite calm the wild flutter of panic in her chest.

She looked up into Thomas's face, searching for any sign of the recklessness she feared. But beneath the easy smile lay something more serious—a careful intelligence that reminded her of his older brothers.

James's hand pressed more firmly against her back. "If Thomas is determined to do this, then we need to plan it properly. No rushing in without thinking it through."

She let her breath out, and the weight on her chest eased a little. She would have to trust him. And tell him everything she could think of that might help.

"I need to tell you about the layout. And about Murphy—he's the one who owns the saloon. He's not like Vincent, but he's loyal to him. Vincent pays him well for my performances, and Murphy doesn't ask questions about things that aren't his business."

Thomas nodded, his expression growing more serious as he listened. "What time does the saloon close?"

"Around two in the morning usually. Sometimes later if there's a big poker game." She closed her eyes, picturing the familiar routine that had governed her life so many years. "Murphy always does a final walk-through before he locks up—checks the main room, counts the till, makes sure all the lamps are out."

"And Vincent's office?"

"It's down a hallway that runs behind the main bar. Before the back staircase at the end of the hall."

Thomas nodded, his expression intent. "So the office is between the main saloon and the back stairs?"

"Yes. About halfway down the hall."

She could almost see him mapping it out in his mind. "What about the lock?"

"Heavy brass. Vincent always made a show of using it, even when he was just stepping out for a moment." The memory of that metallic click made her stomach clench. "He keeps the key on a chain in his vest pocket."

Thomas spewed question after question at her, and she did her best to answer them all. His methodical interrogation reminded her of Robert's legal mind, but with an edge of excitement that was purely Thomas's own. By the time he seemed satisfied, her entire body ached from reliving her life in that place.

"All right." He straightened, that familiar glint of mischief now tempered with something more serious. "I'll leave at first light, get to Virginia City by Monday afternoon. That gives me time to scout the place before the saloon gets busy. I'll decide whether it's best to sneak in while a lot of people are there, or wait till after they close."

The knot in her stomach tightened again. Even with all their planning, the thought of Thomas walking into Vincent's territory made bile churn in her middle. She'd seen what Vincent did to people who crossed him—the quiet threats, the way problems simply disappeared.

As though he could sense this new wave of distress, James's hand moved against her back, a gentle reminder of his presence. "Thomas knows what he's doing," he said quietly, though she could hear the worry he was trying to hide. "And if anyone can talk his way out of trouble, it's him."

Robert cleared his throat. "If you plan to take the letters, I guess we'd better start writing them."

While the others worked out the wording, Rose let her gaze drift out the window. This attempt felt too big. Too impossible without Someone more powerful overseeing every step. She hadn't prayed in years, not really. But maybe…

Before shame could stop her, she shaped a quiet plea. *Lord…if You're as near as they seem to believe, keep Thomas unseen. Keep him safe.*

The words felt strange, like wearing a dress that wasn't hers. And she didn't expect an answer.

Still, the asking eased something tight inside her.

# CHAPTER 13

The bitter wind cut through James's coat as he guided his horse down the slope toward the ranch house, his jaw clenched against more than just the cold.

Snow had been falling since last night, blanketing the Montana peaks in pristine white that would have been beautiful if it didn't spell a hard few days or weeks for their stock. He, Enoch, and Robert had been working with the horses in the meadow pasture all morning, until Robert had gone back to the barn to fetch the ax over an hour ago—a simple task that should have taken fifteen minutes at most. The ice on the creek in the north pasture would be thick by now, and cattle couldn't survive long without water, no matter how much hay they had stored.

As he rode into the barn, Robert's horse stood in its stall, still saddled but sleeping, as though it had stood there a while. The ax hung exactly where it always did, untouched on its wooden pegs.

He couldn't help but growl as he strode toward the house, irritation building with each step.

Four days. Four days since Thomas had ridden out for

Virginia City to retrieve Rose's contract, and the waiting had stretched everyone's nerves thin. The least Robert could do was handle the simple tasks he'd been asked to do instead of—

As he crossed the porch, he forced himself to slow down before easing open the front door.

The sight before him made his gut twist.

Rose sat curled on the leather sofa in the great room, her auburn hair catching the lamplight as she bent over what looked like a book. Robert sat beside her—close beside her—their heads nearly touching as they studied whatever lay open between them. Her green eyes were bright with interest as she pointed to something on the page, and Robert's expression held that same patient attention he'd always given to his books.

The jealousy hit James hard, sharp and immediate beneath his ribs. His hands clenched at his sides as he watched them, so absorbed in their conversation they hadn't even noticed him enter.

Rose's relaxed posture, the way she leaned toward Robert without any of the careful distance she maintained with everyone else, made his chest burn with something ugly and possessive.

The ax. The cattle. His brother had abandoned his responsibilities to sit here playing scholar with Rose while James and Enoch worked in the bitter cold and while cattle stood thirsty in the north pasture. He was probably trying to impress her with his knowledge of legal precedents or some other intellectual pursuit that made James feel like a rough-handed rancher by comparison.

The worst part was how natural they looked together—two minds bent over a shared interest, Rose's delicate features animated with the kind of engagement she never showed when James tried to talk with her. When he attempted conversation, she gave him polite responses and careful smiles. But here she was, leaning into Robert's space as though she belonged there.

The rational part of his mind knew he was being unreasonable—Robert was probably just answering a question she'd asked from one of his law books. But rationality had nothing to do with the jealousy that clawed through his chest like a living thing.

"Robert." The name came out harsher than he'd meant, cutting through their quiet discussion like a blade.

Both heads snapped up. Rose straightened immediately, that familiar wariness sliding back into her expression like a mask. Robert blinked, looking genuinely surprised to see him standing there.

But before his brother could defend himself, the sound of hoofbeats in the yard made James spin.

Thomas was back.

And if God was merciful, he'd have Rose's contract with him.

James stepped back onto the porch as his youngest brother reined in amidst the still-falling snow.

Thomas swung from his saddle, his movements stiff from the long ride. Snow clung to his coat and hat, and his face flushed red from the cold.

But his eyes held a gleam of satisfaction that made James's pulse quicken.

"Did you get it?" James called out, stepping to the edge of the porch.

Thomas patted the front of his coat. "Got it." His grin was sharp with triumph. "Vincent Dunhill is very organized."

Relief flooded through James's chest, washing away some of the bitter jealousy that had just been eating through him. Rose's contract—the key to her freedom—was finally within their reach.

"Thomas!" Robert's voice came from behind him, and James turned to see his brother emerging from the house, Rose close behind him. Her face had gone pale, her green eyes wide with a mixture of hope and fear that twisted inside him.

Thomas pulled a folded paper from inside his coat, holding it up like a prize. "Miss Rose, I believe this belongs to you."

She pressed her hand to her mouth, staring at the document as though it might disappear if she looked away. "You really did it. You got my contract."

Thomas's grin widened despite the exhaustion etched in the lines around his eyes. "Vincent keeps meticulous records. I'll give him that. Your contract was right where you said it would be—filed alphabetically in a leather case marked 'Rose.'"

She reached for the paper. Her fingers shook as she unfolded it, and he had to resist the urge to step closer, to offer her the steadiness she so clearly needed.

But Robert was already there beside her, easily slipping into the role of her confidant and advisor. Rose even tipped the paper for him to better see.

The jealousy twisted in James's gut again, sharp and unwelcome. Here was the moment Rose had been waiting for—the key to her freedom—and she was sharing it with Robert while James stood on the periphery like a stranger.

"Let's get inside." His voice came out a bit too rough. "Thomas looks half-frozen, and we need to read through that document properly."

James pushed open the front door, stepping back to let Thomas pass, but his attention remained fixed on Rose. She clutched the contract against her chest like a lifeline.

The warmth of the great room felt almost shocking after the bitter cold outside, but it did nothing to ease the tension coiled in his chest.

Thomas shrugged out of his snow-dusted coat and moved toward the fire, holding his hands out to the flames. "That's better. I thought I might freeze to the saddle on that last stretch."

Rose sank onto the sofa where she'd been sitting with Robert moments before, the contract spread across her lap.

Robert immediately settled beside her again, leaning in to read over her shoulder with that same focused attention.

He should be grateful Robert was helping her, that his brother's legal knowledge might be the key to her freedom. Instead, all he could think about was how easily she turned to Robert, how she never looked at James with that same trust and reliance.

He remained standing, though restless energy coursed through his limbs. He turned to Thomas. "Tell us what happened. How did you get in?"

Thomas rubbed his hands together, working warmth back into his fingers. "Waited until the saloon was busy—around ten o'clock that night. Slipped in through the front door with a group of miners who'd had a few drinks. No one pays attention to another face in a crowd like that."

He paused to accept the cup of coffee Mrs. Wang pressed into his hands, nodding his thanks before continuing. "Found the hallway Rose described easily enough. The office door was locked tight, but the lock wasn't anything special. Took me maybe two minutes to get it open."

The casual way Thomas described breaking into Vincent's office made James's stomach clench—as though he were discussing the antics of one of the horses in training rather than risking his neck in enemy territory.

"What about Vincent? Did you see him?"

Thomas shook his head, taking a long sip of the hot coffee. "Heard him though. He was in the main saloon most of the evening, holding court at one of the poker tables. Loud voice— you can hear him from halfway across the room."

Rose looked up from the contract, her face pale. "What else did you see? Was anyone there who might have recognized you?"

Thomas shook his head, settling into a chair by the fire. "Just the usual crowd. Miners, a few gamblers, some working girls.

Murphy was behind the bar most of the night, but he never looked twice at me." He paused, studying Rose's expression. "Vincent seemed to be having a good evening—winning at cards, buying drinks for half the saloon. He had no idea anything was happening."

The relief in Rose's eyes made the tension in his chest ease, but only until she turned immediately to Robert, holding the contract toward him.

"What do you think?" Rose's voice was quiet, but there was a catch in it, a note of urgency she couldn't quite hold back. "Can you tell if—it's as bad as I remember?"

Robert took the paper from her, carefully, as if it might crumble in his hands. His brow furrowed while he read, and James, despite himself, edged closer, drawn in by the need to see for himself what had kept Rose bound to that man for so long.

The silence grew thick, broken only by the faint crackle of the fire where Thomas stood, warming himself, glancing over now and then. Rose watched Robert, her attention fixed and fierce, as if waiting for a verdict she'd been dreading for years.

At last, Robert let out a breath and lowered the paper, his gaze moving around their group. "It's much as Rose said. A good solicitor could likely prove it invalid, on account of her age and the state she was in." He looked at Rose then, sympathy plain in his face. "I'm sorry that cad forced this on you."

"Is there anything we can do now?" Everything in James needed to take action.

"I'd like to review it more carefully. Study the exact wording and compare it to other published cases." Robert frowned at the paper. "I'll have my notes ready when we hear back from Father's contacts."

James's chest clenched. It sounded like Robert needed time to focus on the work.

And there were still cattle in the north pasture needing water.

The weight of responsibility pressed down on his shoulders like the snow accumulating on the roof above them. He was supposed to be learning to run this ranch—Enoch would be leaving for England with Mandie next year, and the day-to-day operations would fall to him.

The thought should fill him with purpose, with the satisfaction of stepping into his role as the ranch's future owner.

Instead, all he could think about was how Robert got to be the hero—the one with the knowledge Rose needed, the one she turned to with trust shining in her green eyes. While James would be out in the bitter wind, breaking ice and tending cattle, Robert would be here in the warm house, poring over legal documents with Rose hanging on his every word.

The injustice of it burned in his chest like coals.

He forced himself to focus on what mattered most. Rose's freedom. The cattle's survival. His own petty jealousies had no place in either equation.

"I'm going out to break the ice in the north pasture." He turned to the door, leaving the press of thick silence behind. He didn't let himself look back to see Robert's reaction to the reminder of the task he'd been assigned. Maybe he had his nose so deep in the contract, he hadn't even heard James.

As he closed the door behind him, the cold air hit his face, sharp and clean after the suffocating atmosphere inside. He stood on the porch a moment, breathing deeply, letting the wind carry away some of the bitter frustration building in his chest.

Rose. She was supposed to be *his* particular friend. They'd always had a special connection. Even when he first brought her home from Butte, there had been an awareness between the two of them. A tension she'd seemed to be fighting.

But now...how had Robert stepped in and stolen her attention completely? Sure, she was focused on the contract and how she could be free from that lecher, Vincent Dunhill. But they were all working to help her with that, James included.

Maybe he just needed to find a way to spend extra time with her. A way to remind her of what they'd always had.

Rose was the only woman he'd ever loved, and maybe if she finally allowed herself the chance, she would realize she loved him too.

He simply had to find ways to show her. To win her heart.

The thought crystallized in his mind as he strode to the barn, his boots crunching through the fresh snow. He'd been too passive, too willing to step back and let his brother take the lead simply because Robert had the legal knowledge Rose needed. But there were other ways to help her, other ways to prove his worth.

And more importantly, there were other ways to remind her of what they'd once meant to each other.

The barn felt warm after the bitter wind outside, the scents of hay and horses steadying him. He grabbed the ax from its pegs, hefting its familiar weight in his hands. The tool felt solid, honest—unlike the tangled mess of emotions churning in his chest.

As he headed back to his horse, who stood waiting patiently, a plan began forming in his mind. If he took Rose to some of the places they'd loved as kids, she would remember their bond. They could even create new memories in those familiar spots.

Where had they spent most of their time in the winters?

The old swimming hole. They'd devoted countless winter afternoons there when the creek froze solid enough to skate on. Rose had been fearless on the ice, laughing as she glided across the frozen surface while he'd shown off, attempting jumps and spins that usually ended with him flat on his back. She'd always helped him up, her green eyes bright, her mittened hands surprisingly strong as she pulled him to his feet.

The memory warmed something in his chest that had

nothing to do with the bitter wind. They still had a box full of skates of all sizes. Surely he could make some of them work.

Yes, that would be perfect. Once this storm passed and the ice was safe, he could take her skating again. Show her that he remembered everything about their friendship, that he valued those memories as much as she did.

And the cave they'd discovered halfway up the ridge behind the house—not really a cave, just a deep depression in the rock face, but it had felt like their own secret kingdom when they were children. They'd spent hours there on winter afternoons, telling stories and sharing the cookies Mrs. Wang had smuggled to them.

His grip tightened on the ax handle as he swung into the saddle. He would take Rose to those places. Remind her of who they'd been together before the world had gotten so complicated, before Vincent Dunhill stole her childhood and turned her into this wary, guarded woman who pulled back when anyone drew near.

He'd bring her back to herself. Back to him.

Rose glanced over as the kitchen door opened and Thomas entered the room. But it was his expression that made her pause.

He met her gaze with no hint of the easy confidence he'd shown an hour ago when he told his tale of retrieving the contract.

Instead, his jaw was set in a hard line, and something flicked in his eyes that made her stomach drop.

"What's wrong?"

He glanced behind him, as though making sure they were alone, then stepped closer. "There was something else in Vincent's office. Something I didn't mention in front of the others."

The warmth from the kitchen stove seemed to leach away, leaving her skin cold despite the heat radiating from the cast iron. She set down the wooden spoon she'd been using to stir the stew, her fingers too unsteady to hold it properly. "What kind of something?"

He reached into his coat again, producing another folded paper. "It was in the same file as your contract."

She stepped back before she could stop herself. What more had Vincent done? Her hands wouldn't stop trembling, so she gripped her apron. "What is it?" A quiver slipped out in her voice, no matter how she tried to stop it.

Thomas's expression softened, but he didn't put the paper away. "It's a letter. Or maybe an affidavit. It's about your mother."

The room swayed around her, and she grabbed the counter to keep herself upright. This was it. Somehow Vincent had managed to spread his poison to this new life she'd dared hope for with the Balfours. Without even finding her, he'd stolen her safe haven here with the truth of his horrific deeds—the one he'd threatened to pin on her mother and by extension, her. *Like mother, like daughter.*

"Rose, come sit down." Thomas gripped her arm. Not rough, but strong. Drawing her toward the chairs around the table.

She wanted to pull away, but she had to face this. Had to set the record straight for Mama. Even if it meant the Balfours would make her leave.

Her legs felt like water as he guided her to the chair. The wooden seat felt solid beneath her, but nothing else did—not the familiar warmth of the kitchen, not the safety she'd foolishly allowed herself to believe in.

"What does it say?" The words came out as barely a whisper.

He unfolded the paper and laid it in front of her. "You should read it for yourself."

The words blurred before her eyes, swimming together like ink in water. She blinked hard, forcing herself to focus on the meticulous script she'd always hated.

*Statement Regarding the Death of Lady Catherine Balfour*
    *I, Vincent Dunhill, do hereby attest that Mrs. Margaret Prescott, lady's maid to the deceased, did willfully and with malicious intent administer poison to her ladyship over the course of several weeks in*

*the spring of 1847. Mrs. Prescott confessed this crime to me before our marriage, claiming she needed the jewelry and personal effects she would inherit from her ladyship to better provide for her daughter's future. She begged me to keep her secret, which I have done out of Christian charity and concern for her young daughter. However, should Mrs. Prescott or her daughter Rose ever attempt to contact the Balfour family or make claims against the estate, I feel duty-bound to reveal this terrible truth.*

She pressed her hand against her mouth, fighting the wave of nausea that threatened to overwhelm her.

"Rose." Thomas's voice came from so far away. "Rose, breathe."

She couldn't. The kitchen walls pressed in, the scents of herbs and cooking meat cloying. Suffocating. Vincent's lies stared back at her from the page—lies so carefully crafted, they would seem believable to anyone who hadn't known her mother's gentle heart.

"It's not true." The words tumbled out, raw and desperate. "Thomas, you have to know it's not true. My mother would never—she loved Lady Balfour. She grieved for months after she died."

"I know." His voice was gentle. "Rose, I know."

She looked up at him through the blur of tears. When had they started falling? "You do?"

His expression remained steady, patient. "Rose, we all know your mother loved my mother like a sister. The idea that she would hurt her..." He shook his head. "It's impossible."

The tightness in her chest loosened just enough to let her draw a shaky breath. "Vincent killed her." The words tasted like ash in her mouth, but she forced them out. "He was courting Mama then, visiting the ranch. He had access to the house, to the kitchen. And after she died, Vincent married Mama so quickly..."

Thomas frowned. "Rose, my mother was sick. The doctor diagnosed consumption. I've heard the stories about the blood in her handkerchiefs, though she always tried to hide them."

Of course Lady Balfour had been sick—Rose remembered the long afternoons reading to her, the way her ladyship had grown thinner and weaker with each passing day. But that didn't mean...

"She was sick, yes." Every word felt like torture, but she had to tell the truth. They needed to know. "But after we left, after Vincent married my mother, he told her he'd poisoned her ladyship. When he would come to visit, he added something to her tea. And I think he even left a medicine he told Mama would help her ladyship recover. He made my mother sign this statement. Used it to force her to sing in his theater every night."

Thomas leaned forward. "Rose, you need to tell James about this." His voice wasn't hard exactly. Not mean. Just firm.

*Tell James.* The two words echoed in her mind like a death knell.

The panic that had been building in her chest exploded into something wild and desperate. "I can't. Thomas, I can't tell him this." She should tell him, but the thought of the disappointment on his face. Nay, anger most likely. Would he make her leave? James had never looked at her with anything except affection. If he hated her, if what Vincent had done turned that warmth into loathing...she wasn't sure she could stand it.

"Rose—"

"You don't understand." She pushed back from the table, the chair scraping against the wooden floor. The letter lay there between them, Vincent's poisonous lies staring up at her like a living thing. "If he thinks my mother had anything to do with your mother's death..."

Her stomach heaved. She pressed her hand against her mouth, fighting down the bile surging up her throat. James had been so young when his mother died, but she remembered the devastation in his green eyes, the way he'd cried. How could she tell him her mama had been the one to bring his mother's murderer into their home?

Thomas stood slowly, his movements careful as though she were a spooked horse that might bolt. "Rose, James cares about you. He's not going to believe Vincent's lies any more than I do. But either way, this is an important detail between the two of you. You need to tell him."

*Between the two of you...*

There wasn't anything between her and James. Not anything romantic. No matter how much she wanted more with him.

Even if she weren't a servant, the contents of this letter were exactly the reason why there never could be more.

# CHAPTER 15

The steady whisper of Rose's broom against the wooden floors the next morning had become a kind of cadence, each stroke carrying away not just dust but some of the restless energy that had plagued her since Thomas's return yesterday. Her spirit had been in an uproar all night, but this steady rhythm had finally settled her.

She would work up the courage to tell James about what Vincent had done to his mother eventually. Maybe. But there wasn't a rush. Nothing romantic could ever grow between them anyway. She was merely the hired help. A position she had always held in their home...would always hold.

She paused near the dining room windows, watching a gust of wind kick up a flurry of ice crystals. The storm had finally exhausted itself sometime in the night, leaving the world wrapped in pristine white that made everything look softer, more forgiving.

The sound of boots on the front porch made her tense. It wouldn't be Vincent though, not striding up to the front door. She crept to the doorway to the great room as the front door opened and James stepped inside, snow dusting his shoulders and hat.

Relief eased through her. But too quickly, that other tension coiled in her middle. The one that always came in his presence. James was dangerous in a far different way from Vincent. She couldn't let her heart fall for him any more than it already had.

The familiar green of his eyes, the way snow clung to his golden-brown hair—it brought back too many memories of winter mornings when they'd been children, when seeing James had meant adventure and laughter instead of this complicated tangle of longing and fear.

"Rose." His voice carried a warmth that made her grip tighten on the broom handle. "Perfect timing."

She forced herself to remain still as he approached, snow melting from his coat onto the polished floors she'd just cleaned. The scent of winter air and pine clung to him, both familiar and unsettling.

"I was wondering if you'd like to go for a ride with me."

A ride? Just the two of them? Her pulse quickened. "I—why would you want me to—"

"I thought you might like to get out of the house. See a bit of the place." His smile held that boyish charm, the one that had always made her feel special, chosen. "The storm's passed, and the snow is beautiful. Besides, you've been cooped up inside for days."

Every instinct screamed at her to refuse. Being alone with James was dangerous. Even if she'd made peace about not telling him about the affidavit yet. "I don't think—"

"Oh, you should go, dear." Mrs. Wang's voice from the kitchen doorway made Rose jump. The older woman stepped into the dining room, wiping her hands on her apron, her dark eyes twinkling even more than usual. "You've been working so hard, and the fresh air would do you good. James knows every trail on this mountain—you'll be perfectly safe."

Safe. The word made Rose's stomach twist. She'd never felt less safe than when James looked at her like this, as though he could see straight through all her careful defenses to the girl she'd once been. What she wouldn't do to go back there.

"I really should finish—"

"The floors can wait." Mrs. Wang's tone brooked no argument. "Go bundle up. The exercise will put color in your cheeks."

Rose found herself nodding despite her better sense, caught between Mrs. Wang's gentle insistence and the boyish hope in James's eyes. "I suppose…if it's not too much trouble."

"No trouble at all." James's smile widened, and that genuine pleasure in his expression nearly melted her completely. "I'll get the horses ready while you bundle up."

A quarter hour later, Rose stood in the barn doorway, her coat buttoned to her chin and thick gloves covering hands that trembled with more than cold.

James handed her the reins to a sturdy mare. "You still remember how to ride?"

The question sent her mind tumbling backward through the years. How many times had she and James raced across these very meadows, their mounts' hooves thundering against the summer earth while they whooped with pure joy?

"I think so."

James smiled, warm as ever. "Belle here is a good soul." His voice held that patient tone he'd used to use when he taught her a new skill when they were children. "She won't give you any trouble."

She accepted the reins, and Belle stood perfectly still as Rose approached her left side. Her muscles protested, but her body remembered the motions to haul herself into the saddle. A jolt of memory snapped through her—the creak of leather, the solid warmth of the horse beneath her, the way the world looked different from this height.

James swung onto his own mount like he'd been born there. Which, he practically had been. The Balfour boys had all learned to ride before they learned to walk.

The cold air bit at her cheeks as they rode out of the barn, but it carried a cleanness that made her lungs expand fully for the first time in days. The snow-covered landscape stretched before them.

"This way." James guided his horse away from the cluster of tracks that left the yard, toward a trail that wound up through the pine trees. "I want to show you something."

The familiar cadence of hoofbeats on snow, the sway and rhythm, the way the world blurred past when you gave yourself to the animal's stride, the way Belle's ears flicked forward with interest—it all felt familiar.

But that felt like another life, another girl entirely.

"Do you remember this path?" James's voice carried through the crisp air, and she turned to look at him. Snow dusted his shoulders, and his breath formed white clouds in the cold.

She studied the trail winding ahead of them through the pine trees. She'd forgotten how beautiful the mountains could be in winter, how the silence felt almost sacred beneath the weight of the snow-heavy branches.

She did her best to reconcile the snow-covered landscape with her childhood memories. Everything felt like an echo of a childhood dream—the way the path curved around a massive boulder, the particular angle of the slope.

"I'm not sure." The admission felt like a small failure. "Everything looks so different with all the snow."

James nodded. "It always does. But you'll see—some things never change."

They climbed higher, following a trail that seemed to exist more in James's mind than in any visible path. Belle picked her way carefully through the drifts, her frozen breath lingering in the air.

"There." James pointed ahead, where the trail curved around a stand of snow-laden pines. "Just around that bend."

The memory hit her as they rounded the trees. That dark hole in the mountainside.

The cave. Their cave.

Seeing it again, even buried under snow and ice, sent memories flooding through her with such intensity she nearly gasped aloud.

Countless winter afternoons spent huddled in that rocky shelter, sharing stories and dreams while the wind howled outside. James teaching her to whittle with his pocketknife, the wood shavings curling at their feet. The day she'd cried over her mother's scolding about proper behavior for young ladies, and James had sat beside her, his arm around her, until the tears stopped.

She pressed her mittened hand to her mouth. This place had been theirs—completely, utterly theirs—in a way nothing else had ever been.

They dismounted in silence, the air between them thick with memory. James tied the horses to a pine, then faced the cave. Snow had drifted high at the mouth, but the hollow inside waited, dark and unchanged.

He went first, boots crunching through the crust, clearing the way. The smell hit her as she entered—stone, earth, and that wild, secret scent that had always made this place theirs.

The cave was smaller than she remembered, but wasn't everything from childhood?

Still, the curved walls welcomed her, close and sure, wrapping her in a feeling of home.

"Look." James moved to the back, then brushed snow from a rock shelf. "Still here."

Her heart jumped. Their treasure box—a battered tin that had once held Mrs. Wang's special tea—sat exactly where they'd left it all those years ago. The metal was rust-covered now, but one corner still bore that dent from where James had dropped it years ago while trying to hide it from Will.

Her throat tightened as James lifted the lid with careful fingers. Inside, wrapped in what had once been a piece of his mother's good linen, lay the treasures they'd collected—smooth river stones, a hawk feather, pressed wildflowers that had long since crumbled to dust. And there, at the bottom, James's first attempt at carving—a lopsided wooden horse that had been her most prized possession.

"You kept it all." She shucked her gloves to lift the little horse from its nest of memories. The wood felt smooth and familiar in her palm—and cold—worn by countless hours of play.

"Of course I did." Something in his voice made her look up, and the warmth in his green eyes sent heat spiraling through her chest despite the bitter cold. "I kept everything that mattered."

The weight of his words settled between them, heavy with meaning she wasn't ready to examine. She set the horse back in the tin, her chest too tight to speak.

James pulled something from his coat—a wrapped bundle that smelled like Mrs. Wang's kitchen. "I thought you might be hungry."

The familiar ritual of it made her throat ache. How many times had they shared meals in this exact spot, their voices echoing off the stone walls as they planned adventures or shared secrets?

He spread his coat on the driest section of stone, just as he always had. Why had she never offered her own coat? James wouldn't have let them use it, even if she had.

She settled beside him on the makeshift seat, careful to maintain proper distance despite the cave's cramped confines. The stone beneath them radiated cold through the wool, but James's presence warmed the air between them in ways that made her pulse quicken.

He unwrapped the bundle, revealing thick slices of Mrs. Wang's bread, cheese, and dried apples. The sight of it transported her back so completely she could almost hear their younger voices echoing off the stone walls, could almost see James at eight years old, his face still round with boyhood as he divided everything exactly in half.

"Do you remember when we found the coyote pups?" His voice rumbled soft in the close space.

The memory bloomed in her mind, sharp and sweet. "They were so tiny. All curled up together in that back corner." She pointed to the shadowy recess where the cave curved deepest into the rock. "Their eyes weren't even open yet."

"And you insisted we had to feed them." James's smile warmed his voice. "You were so worried about them."

"Because their mother never came back." The old grief touched her chest—that childhood heartbreak over creatures too small and helpless to survive alone. "We waited for hours."

"Three days." One corner of his mouth tipped. "You made me bring milk and scraps every day for three days before they disappeared."

Rose frowned, studying his face. That wasn't right. Something in his version of the memory felt off, like a melody played in the wrong key. She tilted her head, working to resettle the details in her mind. "No. It was only one day we brought them milk. The second day we found them gone, but we also found the tracks—remember? The mother had come back after all, probably moved them to a safer den."

James paused with a piece of bread halfway to his mouth, his brows drawing together. "I'm sure it was three days. And you were so determined to save them you convinced Mrs. Wang to let us take some of the kitchen scraps."

"James." She turned to face him fully, that old spark of indignation flaring in her chest—the same feeling she used to get when Will would insist he'd caught a bigger fish or climbed a higher tree. "We found them in the morning, right after breakfast. You dared me to explore the very back of the cave, remember? I was scared it might go deeper than we thought, but you said you'd already checked."

"I remember the dare." His green eyes held that stubborn glint. "But we definitely came back multiple times to check on them."

"Once." She held up a single finger, warming to the argument despite herself. "We came back once to give them milk. Then the next day, they were gone. You said their mother probably moved them to a safer den, and I cried because I was worried we'd scared her away."

"Rose, I think I'd remember—"

"You told me a story about a brave mother coyote who carried her babies to a magical valley where they'd never be hungry or cold." She watched his face as the memory settled between them. She could see that nine-year-old boy so clearly, the one who'd tried so hard to comfort her.

James's expression shifted, the stubborn set of his jaw softening into something that looked almost sheepish. "You're right." He set down his bread, running a hand through his hair. "I'd forgotten about the story. You always remembered details better than I did."

The admission spread warmth through her chest—not just because she'd been right, but because of the way he said it. Without defensiveness, without the wounded pride she'd learned to expect from men when their version of events was questioned.

Vincent had never admitted to being wrong. About anything. No matter how small.

"I loved that story," she said quietly. "About the magical valley. I used to imagine finding it myself."

"Maybe we did find it." James's voice carried a gentleness

that made her pulse quicken. "This place always felt magical to me."

Something shifted in his eyes—a flicker of that old intensity that made her pulse quicken. The cave felt even smaller now, the air between them charged with memories and something else she didn't dare name.

She reached for a piece of bread, needing something to do with her hands.

"Do you ever wonder what would have happened?" James's voice was quiet, almost lost in the cave's hush. "If things had been different. If your mother hadn't remarried. If you hadn't had to leave."

The question splashed through her like a stone thrown into still water, sending ripples of longing and regret through her chest. She'd wondered that exact thing countless times during the dark years with Vincent—lying awake in her narrow room above Murphy's saloon, staring at water stains on the ceiling and imagining—praying desperately for—a different life.

A life where she'd grown up here on the ranch, where James's friendship had deepened into something more, where she'd never learned to stiffen at a man's touch or calculate the safest response to every question.

The piece of bread turned to sawdust in her mouth. She forced herself to swallow, to meet his eyes despite the way her heart hammered against her ribs. "I try not to think about it."

James leaned forward, close enough that she could see the flecks of gold in his green eyes, smell the winter air that still clung to his shirt. "Rose—"

"We should eat." She reached for the cheese with shaking fingers, desperate to break the spell of intimacy that threatened to crack open the careful walls around her heart. "Mrs. Wang will worry if we're gone too long."

But James didn't take the hint. Instead, he shifted closer on the stone seat, and warmth radiated from his body like heat from a banked fire.

"Rose." Her name on his lips carried a weight that made her pulse stutter. "I need you to know—when you left, when your mother took you away—it nearly destroyed me."

She couldn't breathe. She'd imagined he might have been sad, might have missed their friendship. But the raw pain in his voice spoke of something deeper, something that matched the hollow ache that had lived in her chest for eleven years.

"James, don't." She squeezed the food in her hands, trying to steady herself. "We were children. We—"

"You were everything to me, and not a day's gone by since then that I haven't missed you. Haven't wondered if I should search for you. Or whether you wanted to be left alone." His voice dropped to a whisper. "I wish I'd gone after you. I wish I'd seen what kind of life you were forced to live and brought you home."

Tears blurred her vision, burning her eyes and fighting to break free from her defenses. How many times had she yearned for someone to come and rescue her from her life with Vincent.

James. She'd dreamed of *James* coming for her. Of him knowing in that wordless way he always had that something was horribly wrong in her world. And not stopping until he'd saved her.

"I'm sorry, Rose." His voice rasped. "I'm sorry I didn't come and fight for you when you needed me most."

She could see nothing through the streaming tears, yet she fought with everything in her to hold back the sobs.

But when James's hand slid under hers, his strong callused fingers wrapping around her own, the touch tore down the last of her barriers.

# CHAPTER 16

The first sob escaped Rose before she could stop it, raw and broken in the cave's hushed silence. The sound echoed off the stone walls, carrying with it eleven years of buried grief and longing she'd tried so desperately to contain.

But James didn't pull away. His thumb traced over her knuckles, steady and sure, the same gentle touch she remembered from childhood scrapes and disappointments. The familiarity of it only made her cry harder.

"I used to lie awake at night." She hiccupped the words. "Wondering if you'd forgotten about me entirely. If any of you even remembered I'd existed."

"Never." The fierce certainty in his voice drew her eyes away from her hands clenched in her lap. His green eyes blazed with something that squeezed her chest even tighter. "Not a single day, Rose. You were always on my mind. I sent letters, but I should have come. I should have known you were in trouble. Should have felt it somehow. Searched every town and mining camp until I found you. I should have brought you home years ago."

Letters? She sniffed, trying to process his words through the haze fear and relief and overwhelming emotion. "You sent letters?"

"Once I found out you were in Virginia City. Every few months at first, then less often when…" His voice trailed off, but she could read the pain in his expression. When she never responded.

Her stomach dropped. "I never received any letters." Vincent would have intercepted any mail that came for her. He'd controlled every aspect of her life, every connection to the outside world. How many letters had James sent that she'd never seen? How many times had he reached out while she'd believed herself completely forgotten? Vincent had stolen even that.

Years of grief, pressed down and hidden, spilled out now in this small stone sanctuary.

James shifted closer, his shoulder a perfect fit as his arm came around her. For a breath, every instinct screamed at her to pull away—to shrink from a man's touch, to measure the danger in each movement.

Vincent had taught her that love was something you earned through perfect behavior. It always felt like God's favor was like that too—contingent on flawless obedience.

But this was James. The boy who carved her wooden horses and spun stories of magical valleys. The man who searched for her, wrote letters she never saw, kept their childhood treasures safe in a battered tin box.

She let herself lean into his warmth, and he wrapped his other arm around her, cradling her in his hold. The safety of it… His heart beat against her cheek through the thick wool of his shirt, steady and sure in a way that anchored her for the first time in years.

"I'm sorry," she whispered against his shoulder, though she wasn't entirely sure what she was apologizing for. The tears, maybe. Or the years of silence he'd mistaken for indifference.

"Don't apologize." His voice rumbled through his chest, vibrating against her cheek. "You have nothing to be sorry for."

She pressed her face closer, breathing in the scent of pine and leather and man, relaxing into the tender strength in his arms—it felt like coming home to a place she'd thought lost forever.

Minutes passed in the cave's sheltered silence, her grief finally fading as his heat seeped through her coat and into her bones. The stone walls that had witnessed their childhood secrets now held this moment too—raw and fragile and more honest than anything she'd shared with another human being since Mama passed. Before that even.

When she finally lifted her head, James's green eyes searched her face. His thumb brushed away a tear from her cheek, the callused pad rough against her skin.

"Rose." Her name was barely a whisper, but it carried the burden of every unspoken word he'd held back through all the years since she'd left.

The cave felt suspended in time, as though the world beyond these stone walls had ceased to exist.

Her pulse thrummed in her ears, and his breath brushed her forehead as he leaned closer, dipping his chin so their gazes locked. "I never stopped loving you."

The careful walls she'd built around her heart trembled, threatening to crumble entirely under the weight of his confession.

"James—" She started to pull back, but his hand cupped her face.

"I know you're scared. I know you have good reason not to trust anymore." His knuckle traced along her cheekbone, and pain glimmered in his green eyes. "But I need you to know that what I feel for you has nothing to do with pity or obligation. I love you, Rose. I've loved you since we were children, and I'll love you until I draw my last breath."

The words she'd dreamed of hearing for so many years crashed over her like an avalanche, beautiful and terrifying in equal measure. Every fiber of her being wanted to sink into his declaration, to let herself believe in the possibility of love without conditions or contracts.

Of love with James.

Fear clawed at her chest with familiar talons. Men said beautiful things when they wanted something. She'd learned that well.

But James had never taken, never demanded. He treated her like she mattered simply because she existed. Like her worth wasn't something she had to prove. He fought for her and was even now working to free her from the contract that had smothered her. Not because she'd done something to earn his protection, but because he cared.

Could God possibly see her that way too? The thought was too big, too good to actually be true. But here, safe on the Balfour ranch and tucked under James's arm, the possibility didn't seem quite as impossible as it once had.

Her hand trembled as she lifted it to rest against his chest, the steady rhythm of his heart strong beneath her palm. The warmth of him seeped through the wool, solid and real in a way that made her throat ache with longing.

Would it be wrong to kiss him? Would it ruin this haven she'd finally found?

Or would it help? If James wanted this from her, it would be easy enough to give to him. He wouldn't press for more than a kiss. She knew that without question. James would protect her. And if this would please him…

Just as she was about to lean in, something in his gaze shifted. Almost like he was pulling back.

She didn't move. Just waited to see what he would do. What he wanted from her.

His hand shifted from her cheek, brushing hair back behind

her ear. The strands stuck to the moisture on her face, but his touch was so full of care.

His rich green eyes held hers, so soft, and almost…smiling. "I don't want you to feel like you have to do or say anything. I just needed you to know how I felt. How important you are to me. I'll be here. No matter what you need. I'll always be here for you."

Another tear trickled past her defenses. Why couldn't she stop crying? And how could this man be so good? As if to prove that point, he captured the drop with the pad of his thumb and whisked it away.

Somehow, she had to thank him. But speaking again would probably make her cry more. So she leaned into him once more and wrapped her arms around his waist. "Thank you." She managed those words, then sniffed back the moisture.

He wrapped her tight, and one of his large strong hands rubbed her back.

She couldn't let herself linger in this hold, or she would fall apart again. When she pulled back, he seemed to understand she had to get up. To leave this place and pull herself back together.

He reached for the bag of food. "Want to finish eating in the saddle?"

"That would be good." She needed to get back to help with the evening meal. Bea had mentioned a warm stew, which would require peeling and slicing potatoes.

As they prepared to leave, Rose cast one last glance at the tin box sitting on its rocky shelf. What if she never made it back to this cave?

"Should we take it with us?" James's deep voice rumbled near her ear.

She glanced up at him, but he stood so close, she couldn't hold his gaze long. "Can we?"

"Of course." He tucked the tin under his arm. "This belongs with you."

The significance of his words settled in her chest—not just about the box, but about everything. The memories, the friendship, the love he'd just confessed. It all belonged with her, maybe had always belonged with her, even when she'd believed herself forgotten and alone.

As they stepped from the cave, the afternoon light seemed blindingly bright after the sheltered dimness. The cold air stung her tear-warmed cheeks, but the bite felt cleansing somehow, washing away the last traces of the storm that had raged inside her.

Belle stood patiently where they'd left her, snow dusting her dark coat. James helped Rose mount, his hands steady at her waist as she settled into the saddle. The brief contact sent warmth spiraling through her, different now after what had passed between them in the cave.

But as James moved to untie his horse, his boot slipped. His foot shot out from under him, his arms windmilling as he fought for balance.

His body twisted as he scrambled to regain his footing, and then he was falling—landing hard onto the rocky ground beneath the snow.

# CHAPTER 17

Ice froze in Rose's veins at the sound James made when he hit the ground—a grunt mixed with a strangled cry.

"Jamie!" She leaped from Belle's back and ran to him. Her boots slipped on the same treacherous patch that had claimed him, but she was already ducked low and caught herself with her hands in the snow. She dropped to her knees beside him, her heart hammering as she took in his position.

He'd landed on his side, his left leg twisted at an angle that looked wrong.

"Don't move." Panic strangled her voice. "Let me see."

He pushed himself up on one elbow, his face pale beneath the flush of cold on his cheeks. "It's fine. Just caught myself on something sharp." But his voice held a strained quality that showed he was anything but fine.

She brushed snow away from the rocky outcropping he'd fallen against, revealing a jagged edge of stone that jutted up like a blade. The sight of it made her stomach clench—he could have been hurt so much worse.

"Your leg." She reached toward the torn, bloody fabric. But

the angle of his knee was likely the worst of the injuries. "Do you think it's broken?"

James tried to shift his weight, testing the injured leg, and his sharp intake of breath told her what she needed to know.

"It might be." His jaw clenched as he attempted to bend the knee. "Hard to tell with all the snow."

Rose's hands shook as she brushed more of the white powder away from his leg. A tear in his trousers revealed a gash several inches long, and something wet gleamed against the dark wool. Blood. Blood seeping steadily into the snow now.

She had to get him help, and quickly. She looked up at his horse, trying to think. How could she possibly get him onto his horse in this condition? They certainly couldn't walk. The distance to the ranch house stretched an impossible distance away. Should she leave him here and go for help?

No. Abandoning him alone in this cold would be worse than trying to move him.

"Rose." His voice was steadier now, though she could see the pain etched in the lines around his eyes. "Help me stand. I can ride if you can get me up."

Every instinct screamed against moving him, but what choice did they have? Her mind raced through possibilities, each one worse than the last.

"Just bring my horse here. I can ride back to the house." His voice sounded a little stronger.

If only his horse weren't so immense. "Belle." Rose glanced toward the mare. "She's shorter than your gelding. Easier to mount."

James nodded. Sweat beaded on his forehead despite the cold. "She's steadier too."

Rose hurried to Belle, then led the mare closer to where James sat propped against the rocky outcropping. Each step felt clumsy, her hands trembling as she gripped the reins. What if she couldn't get him home? What if his leg was broken so badly that moving him made it worse?

She pushed the thoughts away. They had no choice but to try.

"Easy, girl." She positioned Belle as close as possible to James. Once Rose halted her, the mare stood perfectly still, as though she sensed the gravity of the situation.

Blood had soaked through more of James's trouser leg now, a black ring against the brown wool. Her stomach twisted, but she forced herself to focus on what needed to be done. "Can you put weight on it at all?"

James braced his hands against the rocky outcropping and shifted. His sharp hiss twisted her insides.

"Some." His voice came out tight. "Enough to mount, I think."

She moved to his good side, ducking under his arm to wedge her shoulder there. The solid weight of him pressed against her, warm and familiar even now. She could feel the tension in every muscle, the way he held himself rigid against the pain.

"On three." She tried to sound more confident than she felt. "One, two—"

James pushed up from the ground with his arms while she lifted, and somehow they managed to get him standing. He swayed against her, his breathing harsh in the cold air, but he was standing.

Getting him into the saddle proved even more challenging. Belle stood rock-still while Rose positioned herself to give James the most support, but each movement sent tremors through his body that radiated into her own bones. The sharp catch of his breath when his injured leg brushed against the stirrup made her stomach clench.

"I'm sorry," she whispered as he gripped the saddle with white knuckles.

"Not…your…fault." The words came out through gritted

teeth, but he managed a strained smile that reminded her so much of her childhood friend that her throat tightened.

Once he was finally settled, she gathered his gelding's reins and mounted quickly.

Now they just had to get back to the house before James passed out from the pain.

# CHAPTER 18

The worst part wasn't the throbbing in James's leg or the way the wooden walking sticks dug into his armpits with every step—it was the way everyone looked at him like he might shatter.

His left leg throbbed with a steady pulse that matched his heartbeat, the splint heavy and awkward beneath his torn trousers. Doc Morrison had come yesterday and done his usual thorough work—seventeen stitches to close the gash, a proper splint fashioned from pine boards and leather straps to immobilize the break just above his knee. The laudanum had dulled the worst of the pain, but it also turned his thoughts to molasses and made him sleep through most of the daylight hours like an invalid.

He wouldn't take the medicine today. He'd face the pain and fight through it.

The sound of quiet voices drifted from the kitchen, and he hobbled that direction. He needed something—anything—to occupy his mind besides his own frustration.

Mrs. Wang glanced up from where she sat beside a basket of

mending, her dark eyes immediately filling with that careful concern he'd grown to hate. "James, dear, you should be resting that leg."

"I've rested enough." The words came out sharper than he'd intended, and Rose's head turned from where she sat across the kitchen table, something that looked like a shirt spread before her.

The sight of her bent over needlework in their kitchen should have soothed something in his chest, but instead it only reminded him of everything he couldn't do. Couldn't ride out to check the stock. Couldn't help his brothers with the horses. Couldn't even walk across a room without looking like a decrepit old man.

"I need something to do with my hands." He resettled himself on the walking sticks, trying to find a position that didn't shoot pain through his knee. "Something useful."

Mrs. Wang exchanged a look with Rose that made his jaw clench. He was twenty years old, not some child to be managed and coddled.

"Well." Mrs. Wang turned back to her basket. "We were just finishing up the mending for today, but if you'd like to try your hand at stitching, there are some small gowns for Mandie's baby that need hemming."

Baby clothes. They wanted him to sit here sewing tiny garments while his brothers handled the real work of running the ranch. The image of himself hunched over delicate infant clothing, needle trembling in his big clumsy fingers, made something hot and bitter rise in his throat.

Rose bit her lip, and her shoulders shook slightly. She was trying not to laugh at him. The realization sent heat flooding through his chest—not the pleasant warmth he'd felt holding her in the cave yesterday, but something sharper and far more humiliating.

"You know I can't do…" He gestured vaguely at the delicate needlework spread across the table.

Rose looked up at him, and there was definitely amusement dancing in those green eyes. "Isn't there something you've been wanting to get done around the house? Or maybe in the barn?"

The barn. Of course there were always things that needed doing in the barn, but most of them required two good legs and the ability to move without these blasted sticks.

"There's always wood to chop." He spoke harsher than he'd meant to, but the image of swinging an ax, of doing something that required actual strength and skill, made his muscles ache with longing.

Rose's expression shifted, the amusement fading into concern. "That's probably not a good idea yet. Not with your leg."

Of course it wasn't. Nothing he wanted to do was a good idea anymore. He was trapped in this house like some parlor ornament while real men did real work outside.

He was being ill-tempered and petty. Yet between the pain in his leg and the thought of his brothers working out in the weather while he lay in bed, he couldn't seem to fix his rotten mood.

"Guess I can hang those shelves in the barn." He turned and started toward the front door.

As he stopped to pull on a coat, hat, and gloves, Rose's steps sounded behind him. "Mind if I come out too? I'd like a bit of fresh air."

He spun to gauge her expression. Those brows lifted sheepishly—almost hopefully—showed his suspicion was right. She wanted to come out and watch over him like a nursemaid.

"I don't need you to coddle me." He growled the words as he pulled on his last glove and reached for the door.

"Good. I wasn't planning to." Rose's pert tone nearly made him pause.

But he resisted the urge to look back again and pushed through the doorway. If only he could stride across the porch and down the steps. The best he could do was hobble to the edge and turn sideways as he took one careful step at a time, each jarring movement shooting fresh pain through his leg.

Rose waited through his slow progress, but he didn't look back at her. Didn't want to see whatever expression she wore—pity, concern, or worse, that barely suppressed amusement he'd caught in the kitchen.

The barn loomed ahead, its familiar bulk offering the promise of honest work, something that might make him feel like a man instead of an invalid.

Inside, the familiar scents of hay and horses usually soothed his restless energy. Today they only reminded him of all the work he couldn't do. He made his way toward the back wall where the leftover lumber was stacked, each step on the walking sticks a painful undertaking.

"Has there been a fire here?" Rose's voice carried a note of surprise as she stepped into the barn behind him.

James glanced up from the lumber stack, following her gaze to the newer timbers that formed the frame above them. "Early summer. Lightning strike during a bad storm." The memory of that night still tightened his chest—the smell of smoke, the frantic race to save the horses, the sick certainty that they might lose everything their father had built. And then Enoch's injury. "We got the animals out, but lost half the structure."

Rose moved closer, her fingers trailing along one of the replacement beams. "This new section looks like it will last forever."

"That'd be nice." He shifted the walking sticks to ease the pressure under his arms. "Been meaning to get proper organization back in here since, but there's always something more urgent needing attention."

That was the truth of ranch life—always another crisis,

another pressing need that pushed the smaller improvements further down the list. Getting the barn organized had been nagging at him for months, one of those tasks that would make daily work easier but never seemed important enough to tackle when horses needed training and hay needed cutting.

"Where were you planning to put the shelves?" Rose moved toward the back wall.

James pointed with one of his walking sticks toward a section. "There. High enough to add rods underneath for the saddles to hang on."

Rose stepped closer to examine the wall, running her palm along the smooth logs. "I can hold things steady for you."

The offer should have been exactly what he wanted to hear. Instead, it grated against something raw in his chest. Rose helping him because he couldn't manage alone. Rose stepping in to do work that should have been simple for a grown man.

"You sure you want to spend your afternoon playing carpenter?" The words came out way too harsh. Why was he taking his weakness out on Rose?

She turned to face him, and something in her expression made his gut twist. Not pity, exactly, but a careful gentleness that somehow felt worse. "I offered, didn't I?"

He hobbled toward the lumber stack, his walking sticks slipping slightly on the packed dirt floor. The pain in his leg had settled into a steady throb that made every movement clumsy and awkward.

The boards he needed were on the bottom of the pile, of course. He leaned one walking stick against the wall and shifted the upper planks with his free hand. Each piece of lumber felt heavier than it should have, his balance precarious as he tried to maneuver the wood while keeping most of his weight on his good leg. The walking stick slipped again, and he had to grab for the wall to keep from pitching forward.

Rose moved without a word to the other end of the board he

wrestled with, lifting it clear of the pile. Her movements were steady, practical—no fuss or commentary about his struggles. Her kindness in the face of his rudeness only made him more angry with himself.

"Thanks." The word scraped against his throat like sandpaper.

They worked in silence to extract the boards he needed, Rose anticipating his movements like she had when they were children. She'd always been able to read his intentions, to be exactly where he needed her without being asked.

He positioned himself against the wall where the shelves would hang, his walking sticks propped within reach. "If you can hold this level while I mark the spots…" He raised the first board, trying to ignore the way his leg screamed in protest when he moved.

Rose stepped close, her hands steady on the far end of the plank. The scent of her hair—something clean and a little like flowers—drifted toward him. Yesterday in the cave, that same aroma had filled his senses when she'd cried against his shoulder. When he'd confessed his love and felt her melt against him.

Now she was close again, but the intimacy felt different—strained from his frustration and the awkward necessity of needing her help for something he should be able to handle alone.

He marked the first nail hole with a pencil, trying to concentrate on the task instead of the way her proximity made his pulse quicken despite his foul mood.

"There." He lowered his end of the board and reached for his hammer. The tool felt familiar and solid in his grip, at least one thing that hadn't changed since his accident.

Rose watched as he positioned the nail, her green eyes focused on his work with the same attention she gave everything. Something about her steady presence began to ease the knot of frustration in his chest, even as his pride continued to smart.

He swung the hammer, and the satisfying ring of metal on metal echoed through the barn. At least his arms still worked properly. He could still drive a nail straight.

"The other end now?" Rose moved to lift the board again without being asked.

They fell into a rhythm—Rose holding, him marking and nailing. His leg throbbed with each jarring impact of the hammer, but the familiar motions of building something useful helped settle his restless energy. This was work he understood, work that made sense.

As they positioned the second shelf, he stole a glance at Rose's profile. The way she concentrated on keeping the board level, her bottom lip caught between her teeth in the same unconscious gesture she did as a girl when she was focused on a task.

"You know." She didn't look at him as she adjusted her grip. "This reminds me of when we built that tree fort behind the creek."

The memory slid in like a gift. "You mean when you insisted we needed a proper floor instead of just branches?"

"Those branches were slippery. I was afraid someone would fall." A smile tugged at the corner of her mouth. "You said I was being too particular."

"You *were* being too particular." But he couldn't help a smile too. "And we nearly broke our necks when the whole contraption collapsed."

"Your mother was so angry." Rose's eyes sparkled with something that looked almost like fondness. "But Mr. Wang helped us build a much sturdier floor."

It had been perfect. Their secret hideaway with its carefully fitted planks and the rope ladder Rose braided from old grain sacks. They'd spent countless summer afternoons in that fort, planning adventures and sharing the penny candy Mrs. Wang smuggled to them from town.

James positioned another nail, the familiar heft of the hammer steadying in his grip. "Wonder if it's still standing. I haven't been that way in a while."

"Probably not. That cottonwood was already old when we built it." Rose shifted to support the other end of the board as he worked his way across. "But I'd like to see, when the weather's better."

When the weather's better. The casual assumption that she'd still be here when spring came sent something warm through his chest despite his persistent frustration. As though she truly belonged here, as though this was her home again.

The third shelf went up more smoothly, their coordination improving with each board. Rose anticipated exactly where he needed her hands, how to angle the plank so he could reach the nail holes without straining his injured leg.

"There." He drove the last nail home, the sharp crack echoing through the barn. Three sturdy shelves now lined the wall, ready to hold brushes, tins of salve, and all the smaller tack that had been cluttering the barn since the fire. "I'll add the saddle bars and nails for the bridles, then things will be a lot more organized." He motioned toward the wad of leather the extra bridles and harnesses had been reduced to.

Rose frowned at the tack. "Maybe I can give them a good cleaning too."

She moved to the pile and lifted one of the bridles to examine it in the dim light. "Mrs. Wang might have some oil I could use."

"There's a tin in that crate by the door."

As Rose settled on an overturned box with the first bundle of leather straps in her lap, he placed the first nail to use as a bridle hook.

When he finished pounding it in, the sound of a whinny in the yard snagged his attention. His brothers weren't due back for hours.

He set down his hammer and reached for his walking sticks. Unexpected company these days couldn't be good.

# CHAPTER 19

"Stay here." He kept his voice low as he made his way toward the barn door, each step sending jolts of pain up his injured leg. "Out of sight until I see who it is."

He sent a quick glance over his shoulder to make sure she wouldn't argue. Her face had gone pale, her hands stilling on the bridle leather. She understood the danger as well as he did—strangers asking questions, looking for a red-haired woman who'd disappeared from Virginia City.

He positioned himself just inside the barn door where he could peer around the frame without being easily spotted. Two riders had halted in front of the house and now dismounted.

His gut twisted. Tom Holbrook from the mercantile. And was that...? Rufus Clark, owner of the sawmill. What in the snowy mountains were these two doing an hour and a half away from town? They both had businesses to run. Though the sawmill might be slow now that the first big snow had hit.

James glanced back at Rose, who'd come to stand behind him. "It's two men from town. Can you hide here in the barn until they leave?"

Her lips pinched tight, but she nodded.

As much as he'd like to wrap her in his arms and hide her away, he forced himself to turn back to see what their visitors were doing.

The two men stood beside their horses, brushing snow from their coats and looking toward the house with the casual air of neighbors paying a social call. Yet nobody rode an hour and a half through mountain snow in this bitter cold just to be neighborly.

Tom Holbrook called out, his voice carrying across the yard. "Hello! Anyone home?"

James straightened and hobbled out of the barn, plastering on what he hoped was a welcoming expression despite the way his pulse hammered against his throat. Every instinct screamed at him to send these men away immediately, but turning away neighbors would only fuel their suspicions.

"Tom. Rufus." He made his way across the yard, his walking sticks slipping a little in the frozen tracks. "This is a surprise."

Tom Holbrook's weathered face split into a grin. "Heard you'd taken a spill. Thought we'd ride out and see how you were mending."

The casual friendliness in Tom's voice didn't fool him for a second. But he worked for a friendly tone. "That's thoughtful of you both. Long ride in this weather."

"Not too bad once you get moving." Rufus Clark stamped his feet, snow flying from his boots.

"Well, I appreciate the concern." He shifted his weight, trying to ignore the way his injured leg throbbed in the cold. "As you can see, I'm getting around well enough. Doc Morrison did good work."

"That he does." Tom nodded, but his eyes swept the ranch yard with the calculating gaze of a man cataloguing details. "You boys been keeping busy despite the weather?"

"Always plenty to do on a ranch." James forced what he

hoped was a natural smile. "Stock doesn't take care of itself, snow or no snow."

The casual conversation felt like riding a young horse for the first time—at any minute, someone could spook the horse and send them all into a tailspin.

Rufus Clark stepped forward, his gaze drifting toward the barn behind James. "Mind if we take a look at how you rebuilt after that fire? I'd like to see how the new wood matches up with what you had before."

James's blood turned to ice. The barn. Where Rose hid, probably listening to every word through the wooden walls.

"I'd be happy to show you around some other time." He shifted on his walking sticks, trying to position himself between the men and that structure without being obvious about it. "But I'm afraid I'm not up for much walking today."

"Oh, we don't mind doing the looking ourselves." Tom Holbrook was already moving around him. "Won't take but a minute."

Panic clawed at James's throat. He couldn't stop them—not without looking suspicious, not with his leg in this condition. All he could do was follow and pray Rose had found a good hiding place.

"The new timber work is mostly overhead." He hobbled after them, his voice pitched loud enough to carry into the barn as a warning. "Hard to see the craftsmanship from down below."

Tom paused at the barn entrance, glancing back with raised brows. "You sound a little hoarse, son. Hope you're not catching something on top of that leg injury."

He cleared his throat. "Just the cold air."

The two men stepped into the barn, and James forced himself to follow despite every muscle in his body screaming at him to block their path.

The barn looked exactly as he'd left it—his tools scattered

near the new shelves, the pile of leather Rose had been cleaning. But no sign of Rose herself.

His eyes swept the interior, trying not to be obvious about searching for her. She must be in one of the back stalls or the hay loft.

"Fine craftsmanship." Rufus's voice boomed in the enclosed space. "You boys did good work matching the old logs."

James hobbled after them, scanning the shadows at the back of the barn, the stalls where Rose might be hiding. "Enoch did most of the planning. Always had an eye for building."

Both men started to move deeper into the barn, but James stopped and straightened. "Can you come in the house a while? I'm sure Mrs. Wang has coffee on, and probably leftover pie too. Mandie will be thrilled to have visitors."

Tom turned with a smile. "How is Lady Balfour? My wife wanted to come see her, but I thought the ride might be too much for her in the cold."

*Lady Balfour.* A reminder that these two men had known them long enough to be aware of their aristocratic ties. And to remember Rose.

"She's doing well." His throat felt like he'd swallowed sand. "The baby's due in a few weeks. She'll be glad to see you both."

He started back to the barn entrance, praying the men would follow. Each step on the walking sticks felt like an eternity, his ears straining for any sound that might give away Rose's hiding place. A shifted board, a stifled breath, the rustle of fabric—any of it could destroy her.

"Coffee does sound good after that cold ride." Rufus finally turned to follow James.

Relief flooded through him, but he forced himself to keep moving toward the house at the same measured pace his injury demanded. Behind him, the men's boots crunched through the snow, their voices carrying on about the snow and the unpredictability of the mountain weather.

As they reached the porch steps, James's mind raced. How long would they stay? What questions would they ask? And most importantly—what had brought them here in the first place?

Mandie appeared at the front door before they could knock, her face lighting up with genuine pleasure at the sight of visitors. "Mr. Holbrook. Mr. Clark. What a lovely surprise."

James forced what he hoped looked like a natural smile as he climbed the steps. "They rode all this way to check on my leg."

"How thoughtful." She stepped aside to let them pass, her gracious manner reminding him so much of his mother's natural hospitality. "Please, come in out of the cold. Mrs. Wang just put fresh coffee on."

The great room felt stifling after the crisp air outside, or maybe that was just the weight of concern pressing on his chest.

Mrs. Wang appeared from the kitchen, her face wreathed in the polite smile she reserved for company. "Gentlemen, how nice. Come and sit. I'll bring coffee and dried apple pie."

Mandie led the way to the dining room, and they all settled in chairs around the table. James took a spot near Mandie, across from their guests.

Tom Holbrook settled into his chair with a satisfied sigh, brushing the last traces of snow from his coat sleeves. "This is much better. That wind cuts right through you."

James nodded instead of growling. Every second these men lingered in his house was another second Rose remained trapped in that barn, probably huddled behind hay or crammed into one of the back stalls.

Mrs. Wang stepped from the kitchen with a tray laden with steaming coffee and thick slices of her dried apple pie, the familiar scents filling the room. Under normal circumstances, the sight would have made his mouth water. Today, his stomach churned too much.

"Mrs. Wang, you spoil us." Tom accepted his plate with

obvious relish. "My Sarah's been trying to recreate this recipe for years, but it never comes out quite right."

"Secret is in the spices." Mrs. Wang smiled as she handed Tom a mug. "And good apples."

Tom nodded. "I believe it. I still remember the very first time I tasted your apple pie. How long's it been now. Eleven years? Twelve?" He glanced at James, as though for confirmation.

James forced a polite tone. "We moved here fifteen years ago."

"That's right. You boys all came with your mother and your hired help. There was a family who lived with you…what were their names? Mother and daughter, I think."

The coffee turned bitter on James's tongue. Here it was—the real reason for their visit wrapped up in neighborly concern and reminiscences. He forced his expression to remain neutral. "The Prescotts. Margaret was my mother's lady's maid."

"That's it—the Prescotts." Tom leaned forward with the air of a man settling into a good story. "Nice woman, Mrs. Prescott. Always so polite when she came to town with your mother. And that little red-haired daughter of hers—what was her name?"

The room closed in around him. Each word from Tom's mouth was another nail in Rose's coffin, another step toward discovery that could destroy everything.

"Rose." Her name scraped against his throat like broken glass.

Rufus Clark looked up from his pie, his face creasing with interest. "That's right. Quiet little thing, always trailing after you boys. What ever happened to them after your mother passed?"

James lifted his coffee cup again, buying himself a few seconds to think. The bitter liquid did nothing to wash away the taste of fear coating his tongue.

"Mrs. Prescott remarried." Each word felt like a step across thin ice. "A man from back east, I believe. They moved away to start a new life." Would that be enough detail to satisfy these vultures? He wouldn't divulge any more of Rose's story.

Tom nodded, but something in his eyes remained sharp and calculating. "Ah, that makes sense. Fresh start and all." He took another bite of pie, chewing thoughtfully. "Funny thing though —that missing person notice that came through the telegraph office last week made me think of the girl. Red hair, green eyes, about twenty years old. That matches her, doesn't it? Do you know where they moved to?"

His chest constricted as if someone had wrapped iron bands around his ribs. "I couldn't say." He cleared his throat, forcing his voice to remain steady. "We lost touch after they moved away."

He had to get rid of these men. Now.

He pushed his coffee cup and the barely touched plate of pie away from him, then focused on Rufus. "Sawmill closed for the winter?"

The man swallowed a hefty bite as he nodded. "The river's not frozen yet, but business is slow."

James forced himself to nod, though his throat felt tight as a noose. How much more small talk would they have to endure before these men left? Would Rose get too cold in the barn, staying hidden and still?

Thankfully, Mandie carried much of the conversation, asking about people around town. Though she'd only lived here a few months, her genteel upbringing showed through in the polite questions she offered now.

At long last, Tom pushed his empty mug toward the center of the table. "I reckon we'd better be heading back before the weather gets cold again."

Relief flooded through James so strong he had to grip the edge of the table to keep from sagging. He pushed himself upright with his walking sticks, his injured leg screaming in protest after sitting still for so long. The pain was nothing compared to the desperate need to see these men gone, to get back to the barn and make sure Rose was safe.

Mandie walked them to the door, chattering about the weather and extending invitations for their wives to visit when the roads improved. Her gracious manner gave James time to position himself near the window where he could watch their departure.

The two men mounted their horses with the unhurried movements of people who had nowhere urgent to be. Tom Holbrook looked back toward the house once, his gaze lingering on the windows as though he could see through them to whatever secrets lay inside.

James forced himself to remain at the window until the riders disappeared around the bend in the trail, their dark figures swallowed by the snow-laden pines. Only then did he allow the careful mask to slip from his features.

He hobbled toward the door as fast as he could maneuver. He had to get to Rose. Would she be scared?

# CHAPTER 20

*J*ames's walking sticks slipped twice on his way across the yard, but he didn't slow down. The barn door stood exactly as he'd left it—slightly ajar, revealing only darkness beyond. Had she found somewhere warm enough to wait? The temperature had dropped while those vultures sat in his dining room asking their pointed questions.

"Rose?" He called her name softly as he stepped inside, his voice echoing in the hay-scented dimness.

No answer.

His pulse quickened as he scanned the interior, searching the shadows between the stalls. "Rose, they're gone. You can come out."

A rustling came from the hayloft above, followed by the creak of ladder rungs. Relief flooded through him so powerfully, his knees nearly buckled. She appeared at the top of the ladder, hay clinging to her auburn hair and skirt.

"I heard them leave." She climbed down, her movements stiff from however long she'd been crammed into her hiding place.

James hobbled toward her. "Are you all right? You must be half-frozen."

Rose brushed hay from her sleeves, her hands trembling—whether from cold or fear, he couldn't tell. "I'm fine. What did they want?"

The careful control in her voice didn't fool him. He could see the tension in every line of her body, the way she held herself like she was preparing for another blow.

"They were asking about you and your mother." The words tasted like ash in his mouth. "About what happened to the Prescotts after Mother died."

Rose went still, her hands frozen in the act of brushing hay from her skirt. "What did you tell them?"

"That your mother remarried and moved away. That we lost touch." He shifted to get more weight off his leg. "Tom mentioned the missing person notice—said it reminded him of you."

Something flickered across her face—fear, maybe, or resignation. The look of someone who'd been hunted for so long that discovery felt inevitable. "Did they believe you?"

He wanted to lie, to tell her that Tom and Rufus had accepted his explanation and would never think of it again. But the calculating look in Tom Holbrook's eyes had been too sharp, too knowing.

"I don't know." The admission scraped against his throat. "Tom's always been curious about other people's business. But it doesn't matter. We won't let him find you."

Rose nodded, though she wrapped her arms around herself. "I should leave." The words came out so soft he almost missed them. "Before I bring more trouble on your family."

"No." The word came out too rough, sharp enough to make Rose take a step back. He forced himself to breathe, to gentle his voice despite the panic clawing at his chest. "You're not going anywhere."

The fear in her green eyes made something sharp twist beneath his ribs. She looked like she had as a child when she'd broken one of his mother's teacups—braced for punishment, ready to bolt at the first harsh word.

He reached for her arm, half expecting her to pull back. But she let him tug her forward. Let him wrap his arms around her as he kept the walking sticks under his arms for balance.

The warmth of her body against his chest eased something that had been wound tight since those men rode into their yard. She was so small, fragile in a way that made every protective instinct in him roar to life.

"They can't have you." The words rumbled against her hair, fierce and certain despite the fear still churning in his gut. "I don't care what Vincent wants or what contracts he thinks he has. You belong here."

Rose's arms slipped around his waist, careful of the walking sticks, and she pressed her face against his shoulder. The trust in that simple gesture nearly undid him.

Something shifted in the air between them, subtle as the change from winter to spring. He felt it in the way her breathing deepened against his chest, in the slight tremor that ran through her frame. When Rose tilted her head back to look at him, her green eyes held something that made his pulse stutter—not fear or gratitude, but something softer and infinitely more dangerous.

The space between them shrank without either of them moving. Her face was so close he could see the faint dusting of freckles across her nose, could feel the warmth of her breath against his skin. The scent of her hair filled his senses—clean and sweet with just a hint of the hay she'd been hiding in.

"James." His name was barely a whisper on her lips, but it carried the weight of every unspoken word that had passed between them since she'd returned to his life.

He should step back. Should remember that she was still

healing, still learning to trust again after years of Vincent's control. But the way she looked at him—like he was something precious and fragile and worth protecting—made rational thought scatter like leaves in a mountain wind.

His hand found her face, tracing the line of her cheek. She leaned into the touch, sending a warmth through his chest. She felt it too. Her eyes fluttered closed for just a moment before opening again to meet his gaze.

"Rose." Her name came out rough. But the longing inside him...the love he'd carried for her through eleven years of separation and loss...

When her lips parted, an invitation he'd dreamed of for so long, something inside his chest snapped like a rope finally reaching its breaking point.

He lowered his mouth to hers.

The first touch of her lips against his sent heat surging through every nerve in his body. She tasted like apples and coffee and...Rose. Her lips were soft beneath his, warm and yielding in a way that made his head spin.

And then...for a moment...she went completely still in his arms.

His heart stuttered to a halt. Terror crashed through him— had he misread her signals? Had he pushed too hard? Too fast?

He started to pull back. To somehow fix the mess he'd made by kissing her.

But Rose caught his face in her hands, stopping his retreat. "Don't." The word came out breathless, almost desperate. "Please don't stop."

Relief swept through him.

She wanted this. Wanted him.

Heat spiraled through his chest, chasing away the cold fear that had gripped him moments before.

This time when their lips met, there was no hesitation. Rose kissed him back with a sweetness that made his head spin, her mouth soft and warm beneath his. Her fingers tangled in the hair at the nape of his neck, holding him close as though she was afraid he might disappear.

He knew that fear well.

After years of dreaming about this moment, of wondering what it would feel like to hold her in his arms as a woman instead of the girl he'd lost, the reality surpassed every fantasy he'd ever harbored.

Her mouth moved warm and soft beneath his, tentative but willing. When he tilted his head to deepen the kiss, she followed his lead with a trust that made his chest ache.

This was Rose—his Rose—finally in his arms where she belonged.

His walking sticks clattered to the barn floor as he brought both hands up to cradle her face. He wanted more of her, to pull her tight against him and submerge himself in her.

But Rose was precious—fragile in ways that went beyond the physical—and he couldn't let his hunger for her override her needs.

Yet when she moved closer, eliminating the small space between them, rational thought scattered completely. Her body pressed warm and soft against his, fitting into his arms like she'd been made for this moment. The trust in her touch, the way she gave herself to this kiss despite everything she'd endured, made emotion swell in his throat until he could barely breathe.

And that's why he didn't hear the sound of footsteps until it was too late.

"What—"

The voice penetrated his haze, and James jerked back from Rose so fast he nearly lost his balance.

Thomas stood in the doorway, silhouetted by the midday sunlight outside. James could barely see his expression, much less read it. But something in the way Thomas held himself pressed wariness through James's chest.

He was surely taking in the scene—Rose's flushed cheeks, the walking sticks scattered on the floor, the way they'd sprung apart like guilty children caught stealing cookies.

Heat crawled up James's neck as he bent to retrieve his supports, his injured leg protesting every movement. But did it really matter if his baby brother walked in on him kissing the woman he loved?

A surge of annoyance crept through him. Once he had the sticks, he straightened, sending his brother a glare as he propped the supports under his arms.

Thomas stepped farther into the barn, revealing the smirk twisting the corners of his mouth. "Enoch sent me back for a hammer and nails. We need to reinforce the shelter in the north pasture before the next storm hits."

"Hammer's hanging on the wall where it always is." James nodded to the spot. Somehow he kept his voice steady despite the way his pulse still hammered from that kiss. "Nails are in the crate by the door."

Thomas's smirk widened as he moved toward the tools, but something flickered in his eyes when he glanced at Rose. Something that looked almost like…a warning?

The look lasted only a moment before Thomas turned his attention to gathering the supplies.

But an uncomfortable weight settled in James's chest. What had that expression meant?

Rose stood frozen beside him, her cheeks still flushed from their kiss, her breathing slightly uneven.

The taste of her lingered on his lips, sweet and warm, making him want to pull her close again despite his brother's presence. He would wait though. And they needed to talk about this change between them. He had to make sure she didn't feel awkward or uncertain.

No matter what, he had to protect her.

But before James could reach out to reassure her, before Thomas had even gathered all the supplies he'd come for, Rose moved toward the barn door. "I should get back to the house." Her voice sounded strange—too bright, too careful. "Mrs. Wang will be ready to work on the evening meal."

"Rose, wait—" He started after her, his walking sticks catching in the dirt as he tried to hurry.

But she'd already reached the barn door, her steps quick and purposeful, putting space between them with every stride. Then she was gone, disappearing into the bright afternoon light.

He could only stare after her as a knot coiled tight in his gut.

# CHAPTER 21

The truth churned like venom in Rose's middle as she stepped into the barn the next morning. She'd worked hard to avoid both Thomas and James the night before, and again this morning.

But now that the other men had ridden out to check on the stock, she had to talk to James. Had to tell him the details she so desperately wanted to ignore.

Thomas was right. James deserved to know the truth surrounding his mother's death. The truth of how her own mother had been involved, even if unknowingly.

The rich scents of hay and horses filled the air, pulling up the precious memory of James in the cave—the soft promise of his kiss, the way he'd cradled her face like something cherished. She should never have let him kiss her without telling him the truth first. She could not pretend he would accept her. No matter how desperately she'd wanted him to.

She'd been selfish. So ridiculously selfish, just like her mother's actions in bringing Vincent to this ranch all those years ago.

She wouldn't let it continue though. She would tell him now.

Then face the consequences. Even if they required her to leave this safe haven she'd come to treasure.

James stood by the ladder leading to the hayloft, his walking sticks propped against a nearby post as he worked to add more rungs.

The sight of him—so strong despite his injury, so focused on the simple task of making something better—made her chest ache with what she was about to destroy.

He must have heard her footsteps because he turned, and the way his face lit up at the sight of her nearly broke her resolve. His golden-brown hair caught the morning light streaming through the barn door, and his green eyes held that same warmth they'd carried yesterday when he'd kissed her.

"Rose." His voice warmed with a note of pleasure that made her chest ache. "I was hoping to talk to you. I couldn't find you after the evening meal last night."

She'd made sure he couldn't find her. Had rushed through cleaning the kitchen with Mrs. Wang, then claimed exhaustion and retreated to her room before he could corner her for conversation.

"I need to tell you something." The words scraped against her throat like broken glass.

James set down his hammer, concern cloaking his features. "What is it?"

The barn closed around her as the air thickened with the poison of what she had to say. She clasped her hands in front of her to keep them from trembling. The memory of his kiss still burned on her lips—a sweetness she was about to sully forever.

She forced in a breath for courage. "When I was twelve, Vincent ordered me to start singing with my mother. I begged Mama to make him change his mind, and she finally told me why she couldn't. Why she sang all those years, letting all those drunken men leer at her. Why she wouldn't stand up to Vincent even for me." Her traitorous voice cracked on those last words.

Mama had protected her, just not the way Rose had begged her to.

"She said Vincent had confessed to her that he'd killed your mother."

The hammer slipped from James's fingers, clattering to the barn floor with a sound that echoed in the sudden silence. The color drained from his face, his green eyes widening with a shock so complete it made her stomach lurch.

"What?" His voice came out barely above a whisper.

Rose's hands shook as she forced herself to continue. "After we reached Virginia City, Vincent told Mama he'd poisoned Lady Balfour. He said if she didn't sing in his theater, he would tell everyone she had done it instead."

James gripped the ladder rung so hard his knuckles went white. "Vincent killed my mother?"

The raw pain in his voice made tears blur her vision. "I don't know for certain. But he had access to her, didn't he? Because Mama had invited him here. Had let him court her right in your mother's house." The words tasted like bile. "If Mama hadn't brought him to this ranch, your mother might still be alive."

He opened his mouth to speak. Then closed it. When he finally responded, his voice came out desperate. "My mother died of consumption."

The last word hung in the air between them—consumption. Rose had heard that diagnosis so many times in the weeks before Lady Balfour's death. Everyone had believed it. *She* had believed it.

Until Mama's trembling confession in that cramped Virginia City room.

"That's what everyone thought." Rose's voice came out steadier than she felt. "But Vincent told Mama he'd been slipping poison into her tea for weeks. Small amounts, so it would look like a wasting illness. He said..." She swallowed against the tightness in her throat. "He said it had been easy because Mama let him visit so often."

James turned away from her, his shoulders rigid beneath his coat. He clung to the ladder with both white-knuckled hands.

She had to finish it all. Had to hand over this incriminating letter. She sucked in another breath for fortitude. "When Thomas went to get the contract, he also brought back a letter." Her throat constricted around each word. "It's a blackmail note Vincent had prepared to use against Mama if she ever tried to leave him."

James turned back to her, his face drained of color, his green eyes holding a blankness she'd never seen in him.

Her fingers trembled as she reached into her apron pocket. The paper burned like fire against her skin—this tangible proof of Vincent's evil, of her mother's entrapment, of Lady Balfour's murder.

She'd avoided looking at it since Thomas gave it to her. Hadn't been able to force herself to unfold the pages again and see Vincent's careful handwriting detailing his crime.

She pulled it free and extended it to James. "Here."

He stared at the paper in her hand for a long moment, as though it might poison him if he touched it. Then his fingers closed around it—those strong, capable hands that had held her so gently yesterday now gripping the evidence of his mother's murder with white-knuckled fierceness.

But he didn't open it. Didn't unfold the pages.

He just stood there, holding the letter while his gaze drifted past her shoulder into the shadowy depths of the barn. His chest rose and fell with shallow breaths that spoke of barely controlled emotion.

The silence swirled between them, thick and suffocating. She wanted to fill it with explanations, with apologies, with anything that might ease the dreadful stillness radiating from him.

But what words could possibly matter now? She'd just told him that her family—her mother's poor judgment and desperate choices—had brought a killer into his home. Had stolen his own mother from him.

"I'm so sorry." The words felt pathetically inadequate. But nothing would bring his mother back.

Each second dragged like hours while she stood there waiting for him to speak. To say something. Anything. Her chest tightened until breathing felt like trying to draw air through wet wool.

Like stone, James stared into the distance. The muscles in his jaw worked like he was trying to form words, but nothing came out. Only that terrible, crushing silence.

She'd expected anger. Had braced for it, actually—for him to turn on her with accusations, to demand to know why she'd kept this secret so long, to order her off the ranch and out of his life forever.

That would have been easier somehow. Cleaner. Like ripping off a bandage instead of peeling it back slowly, tearing away layer after layer of skin with it.

But this was worse than any rage could have been.

She had to get out of here. Had she given him enough time to ask questions? To rail at her if he wanted to?

She took a step back. "I...I'm sorry." The poison of her words bled into the air around them, choking and dark.

James still didn't speak or look at her, so she backed again. Her lungs screamed for air, for relief from the oppression of this barn.

She spun and ran for the door.

# CHAPTER 22

James couldn't think of the pain in his leg. Not now.

The weight in his chest felt far heavier, pressing down with every breath, until it was worse than the throbbing in the broken bone.

He stood in the barn. Incapable of moving. No noises drifted in except for the sounds of dust settling and the faint trace of Rose's footsteps already fading. The letter in his fist was crumpled and damp from his sweat.

He couldn't let go, as if the words themselves might vanish if his fingers loosened their grip.

Vincent Dunhill had murdered his mother.

The thought circled, again and again, refusing to tuck itself away or make sense. For years, he'd believed what everyone said—consumption, the wasting disease. The blood on her handkerchiefs. The way she faded to near nothing in those last weeks.

He'd only been nine then. Old enough to watch her slip away. Young enough to trust the doctor's quiet explanation and not wonder what lay beneath it.

But poison. Vincent had *poisoned* her.

The barn door creaked open, and his muscles tensed. Rose, coming back to—

"James?" Enoch's deep voice cut through his spiraling thoughts. "What's wrong?"

He turned to his brother standing in the doorway, his broad shoulders blocking the morning light. He studied James with the same steady gaze he used on a limping colt, patient but thorough, taking in every sign of hurt.

"I..." The words stuck in his throat like broken glass. How did he even begin to explain this?

Enoch stepped closer. "You look like you've seen a ghost."

Close enough. James forced his fingers to loosen their death grip on the letter, holding it out toward his brother. "Rose just told me something. About Mother."

Enoch took the paper, his expression shifting from concern to wariness. "What about Mother?"

"Vincent Dunhill killed her." The words came out flat, emotionless, like he was reporting the weather instead of confessing the worst truth he'd ever spoken. "Rose says he poisoned her. Then threatened to say her mother did it if she and Rose didn't sing in his theater."

His brother went completely still, his gaze dropping to the paper.

Shock radiated between them, battering James's chest, while Enoch stared at the folded letter in his hand.

Enoch's fingers tightened on the note until the edges crumpled. The muscles in his jaw worked, and something dark flickered across his face—something James recognized from the rare times his brother let his composure slip.

"Read it." James's voice came out hoarse. "It's a letter Vincent wrote to blackmail Rose's mother, if she ever tried to leave him."

He unfolded the letter, slow and careful, as though the paper itself might bite. Quiet pounded hard around them while Enoch's eyes moved across the page.

He studied his brother's face, searching for...what? Shock? Rage? Some mirror of the numbness that had settled in his own chest like frost creeping across a windowpane?

But Enoch's expression didn't change, except for a tightening at the corners of his eyes. A storm gathering. When he finally looked up, his blue gaze held a coldness James had rarely seen.

"He deserves to hang." Enoch's words came out low, measured, but underneath them ran something as lethal as lightning. "I'm not sure if he actually poisoned Mother. I remember her being sick, and the doctor never questioned her illness. But Vincent Dunhill deserves to hang for what he's done to Rose and her mother all these years."

The coldness in his voice matched the ice spreading through James's veins. His brother—steady, controlled Enoch who rarely let emotion override reason—was talking about hanging a man.

And James understood the feeling.

Under his own frozen horror, a fire had caught—a coiling, bitter smoke in his belly, anger sharp as ice.

Vincent had been in their home. Had played the courteous guest and lied with every word. All the while, he'd been killing their mother. Bit by bit. Slow, deliberate poison.

"Rose thinks it's her fault." The words scraped out of him. "Because her mother brought Vincent here. Because—"

"That's ridiculous." Enoch's tone sharpened. "Rose was a child. Her mother was a victim."

That was true. Of course it was. Rose bore no blame for Vincent's evil.

But the look on her face when she'd spoken haunted him— the way guilt and fear had stripped her raw, like she could never believe herself innocent.

He'd stood there, wordless, while she apologized for what she could never have caused, while her eyes flicked up at him, braced for his judgment. Braced for him to condemn her for her mother's choices. For Vincent's crimes.

His chest tightened. He had to go after her. Had to tell her—

"Where is she now?" Enoch's question pulled James back.

"She ran out." He grabbed for his walking sticks, pain crackling up his bad leg. "I need to find her. I need to tell her—"

"Tell her what?" Enoch's hand closed around James's arm. "James, look at me."

He forced himself to meet his brother's gaze, though everything in him screamed to go after Rose. To find her before she convinced herself that he blamed her.

"What are you going to say to her?" Enoch's voice carried that particular tone he used when he was trying to talk James down from something reckless. "Have you thought this through?"

Thought it through? His mother had been murdered. Maybe. Rose had been living with that knowledge for years, trapped by Vincent's threats. And he'd just stood there, more lifeless than one of his carvings, while she apologized for something that wasn't her fault.

"I need to tell her it's not her fault." The words came out rough, desperate. "I need to tell her I don't blame her, or her mother, for what Vincent did."

Enoch gave a single nod. "Good. Tell her I don't either. None of us would possibly think that."

Something in James eased—a brittle knot inside him loosening enough to let him breathe. "Thank you."

Enoch folded the letter and handed it back to his brother. "We need to show this to Robert. He'll know what legal weight it carries."

But the words felt distant. Rose mattered more than anything right now.

He had to find her.

He pulled free of Enoch's grip and hobbled toward the barn door. "I have to go talk to her."

"I have to head up to the high pasture. Tell Rose we'll all talk through this tonight."

James nodded but didn't slow or turn.

As he crossed the yard to the house, his walking sticks bit into the packed snow. The cold helped numb the pain in his leg though.

Where would Rose have gone? Her room, most likely. Or maybe the kitchen, where she always seemed to retreat when she needed the comfort of familiar work.

As he worked up the porch steps, Enoch rode out of the yard, his saddle weighed down with an extra saddle bag—the supplies he'd forgotten earlier, no doubt.

James pushed through the front door, his breath coming hard from the exertion and the storm raging in his chest. The great room stretched before him, dim after the bright light outside.

Then he saw her.

Mandie stood—no, not stood. She *bent* over the back of the couch, her knuckles white where they gripped the wooden frame. Her body curved forward, rigid and unnatural, like every muscle had locked in place.

"Mandie?" Fear twisted in his chest. What was wrong with her?

She didn't answer. Didn't even turn her head. Just stayed frozen in that terrible stillness, her breathing shallow and controlled in a way that set off alarm bells in his head.

He moved toward her as fast as the walking sticks would let him. "Mandie, what's wrong?"

"Don't—" The word came out strangled, barely audible. "Don't touch me."

He stopped an arm's length away, his pulse hammering. Her

face had gone pale as milk, and a sheen of sweat dampened her forehead despite the cool air in the room.

The silence stretched, broken only by her careful breathing. His own mind had clouded over. He tried to think of how to help her, but coherent thoughts wouldn't form.

Then her shoulders loosened—just a little. The rigid curve of her spine eased, and she released a longer breath.

Whatever had gripped her seemed to be passing. The tension in the room shifted, and James finally found his way through his foggy panic. "Is it the baby?"

She nodded, slowly straightening. Her hand moved to her rounded belly, pressing there as though she could hold the child inside through sheer will. "I think... I think it might be time."

*Time.*

The word ricocheted through his thoughts, scattering everything else.

"I'll get Mrs. Wang." He should have done that the instant he saw Mandie in pain.

He started to turn, but another thought struck him.

*Enoch.* Maybe he would still be within calling range.

James spun back toward the door, calling out for Mrs. Wang as he hobbled. When would Mandie's next pain hit? Would she be all right until he came back inside?

As soon as he stepped onto the porch, he bellowed as loud as he could muster. "Enoch!"

There was no sign of his brother on the trail leading away from the house. But still, he shouted with everything in him. "Enoch!"

Two more calls didn't bring sight of his brother riding back, so James turned back.

He'd get Mrs. Wang first. Then he would figure a way to ride to his brothers. Enoch needed to be here with his wife, and someone had to ride for the doctor.

When he stepped into the house, Mrs. Wang was helping Mandie down the hallway toward the bedchamber she and Enoch shared. Good.

He hobbled that direction to see if they needed him to help with anything. If not, he'd ride for his brothers.

Mrs. Wang glanced back as he approached. "I'll take care of her. Go fetch your brothers. Someone needs to get the doctor."

He nodded, already turning back toward the door. But a final thought made him pause. "Is Rose in the kitchen?" She would want to know about Mandie. Would want to help.

The older woman's voice drifted from Enoch and Mandie's chamber. "No, dear. I heard her go upstairs a while ago."

His chest tightened. She'd retreated to her room after their conversation in the barn—of course she had. He'd not said a thing, done anything but gape at her, and now she probably thought he blamed her.

He hobbled to the bottom of the stairs, gripping the newel post as he called up. "Rose! The baby's coming—Mandie needs help. Can you come down?"

Quiet greeted him from the upstairs hallway.

Not the sound of her door opening, not footsteps on the floorboards above. Nothing.

She was probably too upset with him to answer. Too hurt to want to help, or maybe she simply hadn't heard him.

He tried once more, louder this time. "Rose! Mrs. Wang needs you."

He still didn't hear her, but he couldn't wait—Enoch had to know about his wife, and every second counted.

But the moment he arrived back with Enoch, he would find Rose. He would make her understand that he didn't blame her, that nothing Vincent had done could ever change how he felt about her. He'd get down on his knees if he had to, broken leg and all.

He turned and started back to the door, determination settling into his bones alongside the worry. First Enoch. Then Rose.

He wouldn't fail either of them.

# CHAPTER 23

The cold air stung James's face as he hobbled down the porch steps. The walking sticks bit into the packed snow, threatening to slip out from under him twice before he reached the pasture near the barn where his gelding stood, head lowered against the wind.

Too bad James couldn't slip a bridle on the animal and go. But he'd have enough trouble riding in a saddle—bareback would be torture. Peanut was well-mannered enough to let James slip a halter on and lead him to the barn.

Getting the saddle onto the animal's back proved more challenging than he'd anticipated. His injured leg refused to cooperate, and balancing on the walking sticks while hefting leather and wood took three attempts before he finally managed it.

Sweat dampened his shirt by the time he'd cinched the girth strap. His hands shook—whether from exertion or the panic still coursing through his veins, he couldn't say. Every second that ticked past felt like an eternity. Was Mandie all right? How long would the pains last before the baby came?

Mrs. Wang helped neighbor women when their times came,

but James had never been around during the delivery of a child. Not even Robert's or Thomas's.

Once saddle and bridle were secure, he led the gelding out of the barn to the pile of logs that needed to be split into pieces small enough for the cookstove.

Mounting proved even worse than saddling. By the time he'd finally hauled himself into the seat with his legs draped over each side of the horse, his entire leg burned, and his vision had gone blurry at the edges.

He just had to get to his brothers…

He gripped the reins and nudged Peanut forward with his good leg, each jarring step sending fresh waves of agony up his thigh. The splint dug into his flesh through his trousers, and he clenched his jaw against the urge to cry out.

The trail stretched ahead, winding around snow-heavy pines. His brothers had planned to ride out to check the stock in the far pastures, which meant they could be anywhere within a two-hour radius. But Enoch mentioned the high pasture, so that's where he'd start.

James's hands shook on the reins as he guided Peanut around a large boulder jutting from a slope on his right. The cold air burned in his lungs with each breath, mixing with the pain searing through his leg until he couldn't tell where one ended and the other began.

Every few minutes, he called out Enoch's name. He didn't have the strength to yell for all his brothers. Surely if any of them heard his voice, they'd come riding to him.

Peanut's hooves struck the frozen trail with jarring regularity, each impact sending fresh bolts of fire through the broken bone. The splint felt like it was cutting straight through skin now, though he couldn't tell if that was real or just his body's way of screaming at him to stop.

Each jolting breath became a petition, matching the rhythm of his gelding's stride. *Keep Mandie. Keep the child. Keep Rose.*

As the trail wound upward, snow drifted deep in places, forcing Peanut to pick his way carefully around the worst of it. Each time the horse lunged through a deeper patch, the impact shot through James's broken leg like lightning.

He couldn't stop. Mandie needed help. The baby—

"Enoch!" His voice came out hoarse, barely carrying above the wind that whipped through the pines. The cold sliced through his coat, scraped at his skin, made his grip on the reins almost numb—but he forced out another shout. "Enoch!"

Nothing answered him but the whine of wind through snow-laden branches.

He pushed on, the cold seeping through his coat and numbing his fingers on the reins. How long had he been riding? Fifteen minutes? Thirty? Time had become as unreliable as his ability to think through the pain.

The high pasture opened ahead, a broad expanse of snow-covered meadow ringed by dark pines. His brothers' horses stood tied near the far tree line, and the men moved among the cattle that dotted the white expanse like dark boulders.

Relief flooded through him so fierce his arms trembled. "Enoch!"

One of the distant figures turned, and even at this distance, he couldn't miss his elder brother's broad shoulders. Enoch lifted a hand, then started toward him at a jog.

Enoch's long strides ate up the distance between them, and James's chest loosened enough to draw a proper breath. His brother's face was all concern as he closed the final gap.

"Mandie." The word scraped out of James's throat like gravel. "She's in labor. Mrs. Wang's with her, but we need the doctor."

Enoch's face paled. "I just saw her. She was..." He spun, then sprinted to his horse, as fast as the deep snow would allow.

James stayed in the saddle while his brothers mounted. Enoch, of course, tore off toward the house, with Thomas moving only a little slower. He'd volunteered to head straight to town for the doctor.

Robert seemed to be the one assigned to ride back with James, ready to play nursemaid if needed.

His brother reined alongside James as they started back toward the ranch. The silence stretched between them—not uncomfortable exactly, but weighted with everything left unsaid.

The pain settled into a rhythm that matched James's heartbeat. He'd pushed too hard, ridden too far on a bone that was supposed to be resting. Doc Morrison would have his hide for this.

But what else could he have done? Left Mandie without help? Failed to fetch Enoch when his brother's wife was bringing their child into the world? Nor could he have sent Rose out to get lost in the snow.

His gelding stumbled in a drift, and fresh agony shot up James's thigh. He gritted his teeth against the cry that wanted to tear free, his fingers tightening on the reins until his knuckles ached.

"You all right?" Robert's voice cut through the wind.

"Fine." The lie came out rough.

His brother didn't call him on it. A small mercy. But the look Robert shot him said he wasn't fooled.

The trail wound downward through the pines, each step carrying them closer to the ranch house. Closer to Mandie and whatever was happening there. Closer to Rose, who he still needed to find, to talk to, to explain—

His hands were frozen around the reins, even in his gloves, and he couldn't tell anymore if the shaking came from cold or pain or both. He forced himself to focus on breathing—in, out, in, out—to keep from passing out.

"James." Robert nudged his horse closer. "You're white as snow. Maybe we should stop—"

"No." The word came out sharp. But he didn't have the strength for kindness. "Mandie needs us there."

And Rose. He needed to find Rose. Needed to tell her—what? Even that detail seemed blurry now.

Best he stop thinking and hone his focus to surviving this ride back to the house.

# CHAPTER 24

As James opened his eyes, he squinted against the fog clogging his head. His mouth tasted like copper and something bitter, and his leg throbbed with a dull ache that pulsed in time with his heartbeat.

He blinked, trying to force the world back into its proper shape.

The last clear memory he could grasp was riding—Peanut's jarring gait, the urgent need to get help for Mandie, the cold cutting through his coat, Robert beside him on the trail. When had he come inside?

A chair creaked somewhere to his left, and he turned his head. The movement sent the room tilting sideways until he had to close his eyes against the nausea.

"You're awake." Robert's voice cut through the haze.

He forced his eyes open again, slower this time. His brother sat in the corner, legs stretched out in front of him, arms crossed over his chest. The afternoon light through the window behind him made it hard to read his expression, but something in the set of his shoulders said he'd been there a while.

"Mandie." His mouth felt too thick, and his voice rasped like his throat had been dragged through a desert.

Robert leaned forward, elbows on his knees. "The doctor's with her now. Mrs. Wang and Enoch too. Thomas is around if they need a runner."

The words should have eased the knot in his chest, but his insides only twisted tighter. He tried to push himself up, but his arms felt like they'd been filled with sand, and the room spun fast enough to make his stomach lurch.

"Easy." Robert was on his feet now, one hand pressed against James's shoulder. "You need to take it easy."

"I have to—" But what did he have to do? The answer slipped away before he could catch it, dissolving like smoke in the fog filling his head.

Robert's grip on his shoulder stayed firm, anchoring him to the bed even as every muscle in his body screamed to move. He tried to focus on his brother's face, but the edges kept blurring, dissolving into the haze that wrapped around his thoughts.

"What happened?"

"You made it about halfway back before you practically passed out in the saddle." Robert's voice carried that matter-of-fact tone he used when delivering bad news. "By the time I got you to the house, you were out of it from the cold and pain. Enoch and I had to carry you to bed."

Fragments of memory flicked through—the jarring impact of Peanut's hooves, Robert's voice cutting through the roar in his ears, hands gripping him as the world tilted sideways. Nothing solid. Just impressions, like trying to catch water in his fists.

"I gave you laudanum." Robert settled back into the chair. "You finally slept easier after that."

That explained the cotton stuffing his head, the way his thoughts kept sliding away before he could hold them. The bitter taste coating his tongue.

He tried to push through the fog, to grasp something important hovering just out of reach. Something he needed to do. Someone he needed to find.

*Rose.*

Her name sliced through the laudanum haze, bringing with it a rush of fragmented images—her face in the barn, pale and stricken. The letter crumpled in his fist. Her voice breaking as she apologized for something that wasn't her fault.

"Rose." He forced the word out, though his tongue felt thick and clumsy. "Where is she?"

Robert's expression shifted, something crossing his face that James couldn't quite read. His brother looked away, toward the window, then back again. "She left."

*Left...* James blinked, trying to force his thoughts into some kind of order. Left the room? Left the house? "What do you mean?"

Creases weighed down the edges of Robert's eyes. "She left, James. We found a note on her bed."

*No.* The denial roared through him, burning away some of the smoke in his head. Not again. He couldn't lose her again. Not like before.

The memory pressed through him—waking up on a morning much like any other, sunlight streaming in his bedroom window. He'd been nine years old, and the world had still felt like a place where good things could happen if you wanted them badly enough.

He'd padded down to the kitchen in his nightshirt, expecting to find Rose already there, helping Mrs. Wang with breakfast. They'd made plans the night before—something about exploring the creek bed, looking for interesting stones to add to their treasure box. She'd been trying to distract him from missing his mother, and he'd been grateful.

But Rose hadn't been there.

Mrs. Wang turned from the stove, and something in her face

had made his stomach drop even before she spoke. She'd set down her wooden spoon and opened her arms, and he'd gone to her without understanding why his feet felt so heavy.

She drew him onto her lap—he'd been small enough to fit comfortably—and her voice had been soft when she'd told him. Rose and her mother left in the night. Gone to start a new life with Mrs. Prescott's new husband. They wouldn't be coming back.

He'd sat there in Mrs. Wang's warm kitchen, surrounded by the familiar smells of breakfast cooking, as his world cracked apart.

No goodbye. No warning. Just…gone.

And he'd never stopped missing her.

That couldn't be happening again. He wouldn't let it.

Robert reached into his pocket and pulled out a folded piece of paper. The sight of it made bile rise up his throat.

"Give it to me." His hand shook as he reached for the note, his fingers clumsy and uncooperative. As he opened it, the paper felt too light, too fragile to carry the weight of what it represented.

He forced his eyes to focus on the words, though they swam in and out of clarity. Rose's handwriting, neat and careful despite the obvious haste.

*I'm sorry, but I need to leave. It's best I not burden you with my presence any longer, considering the unwanted memories having me in your home will bring on. Thank you for your kindness. I wish you all the best.*

The words blurred as he read them a second time, then a third. Each pass brought fresh pain that had nothing to do with his broken leg.

She thought she was a burden. Thought he blamed her for what Vincent had done.

And he'd let her believe it.

He'd been so caught up in his own shock, in processing the

horror of his mother's possible murder, that he'd failed to give Rose the one thing she needed most.

Love. Unconditional love.

The fog in his head burned away under the force of panic flooding his veins. He pushed himself onto his elbows, fighting past the tilting of the room and the screaming in his leg. "When? When did she leave?"

"We're not sure exactly. I found the note after we got you settled."

It could have been any time after she'd fled the barn. Hours ago maybe.

"Did she take a horse?"

Robert shook his head. "I don't think so. None are missing from the barn or the closest pasture."

She'd been walking out in the cold for hours then, with nothing but whatever she could carry. No horse, no supplies.

His fault. This was his fault.

And he had to fix it. Now.

He swung his legs over the side of the bed, his vision graying at the edges as blood rushed to his head. The splint on his leg felt like an iron shackle, but he reached for his walking sticks anyway.

"James, what are you doing?" Robert stood, his hand already reaching for James's shoulder.

"Going after her." The words came out steady despite the way his hands trembled on the walking sticks. He couldn't let Rose disappear from his life again. Couldn't let her believe for one more second that he blamed her or her mother for Vincent's sins.

"That's not a good idea. Not in your condition."

James met his brother's gaze, forcing his thoughts to find clarity again. The doctor was here with Mandie. Mrs. Wang and Enoch were with her too. Thomas or Robert could run for anything they needed.

They didn't need him. But Rose did.

He pushed himself up to his good leg, blinking back the dizziness that threatened to pull him under again. His injury screamed. But he'd ridden through worse to fetch his brothers. He could manage a wagon ride to find Rose.

He met Robert's gaze. "I'm not sure I can ride astride, but maybe you can help me hitch the team."

Robert's jaw tightened, that stubborn look settling over his features that meant he was about to dig in his heels.

But, at last, he sighed. "Thomas and I are going with you then. We might need all the help we can get."

# CHAPTER 25

The cold had seeped so deep into Rose's bones that even the memory of warmth felt like something from another life.

She pressed herself deeper into the shadows across from the livery, clutching her carpetbag against her chest. If only it could shield her from more than just the wind. Three hours of walking through snow had left her legs trembling and her feet numb inside her boots. The single bag she'd arrived with—the same one she'd carried from Virginia City all those weeks ago—felt heavier now than it had when she'd left the ranch.

Left James.

The thought speared fresh pain through her chest, sharper than the bitter wind cutting down Walnut Springs's main street.

She'd done the right thing. She had.

James deserved better than the constant reminder of how her mother had brought his mother's killer into their home. Better than looking at her face every day and remembering that awful truth.

Even if leaving him felt like tearing out her own heart.

Across the street, the livery remained frustratingly busy.

Two men stood near the entrance, their voices carrying as they discussed horse prices. Another emerged from inside, leading a gray mare by the reins. She needed them all to leave. Needed just the proprietor alone so she could buy a mount without drawing attention, without anyone else remembering the red-haired woman who'd come through Walnut Springs on foot.

The memory of hoofbeats thundering down the trail behind her hours ago still made her pulse quicken. She'd barely had time to throw herself into the trees before the rider had passed —Thomas, she'd recognized him even at a distance by the set of his shoulders, the way he rode like he'd been born in the saddle. His horse had been running hard, foam flecking its neck, heading toward town with urgent purpose.

Coming after her, most likely.

The thought should have made her feel special. Wanted.

Instead it only twisted the knife already lodged in her chest. One of the brothers had come after her, yes. But her heart craved for that brother to be James.

Of course he couldn't ride with a broken leg though.

The ache in her chest intensified until she had to press her gloved hand against her ribs. She could still feel the warmth of his arms around her in the barn yesterday, still taste his kiss. The way he'd looked at her, like she was something precious and worth protecting—

She'd destroyed all of that by telling him the truth.

The image of his face this morning haunted her. The way all color had drained from his skin, the terrible stillness that had settled over him as her words sank in. She'd watched something die in his eyes, watched the warmth that had always been there for her flicker and go cold.

He hadn't said a word. Hadn't told her to leave or stay. Just stood there gripping that letter while she apologized and fled like the coward she was.

A gust of wind whipped down the street, spiraling snow

devils across the packed dirt. She hunched deeper into her coat, but the cold had already worked its way through the wool. How much longer could she stand here waiting?

The boarding house down the street beckoned with its promise of warmth and shelter. She could see lamplight glowing in the windows, could almost smell the coffee and hot food that would be served in the dining room.

The temptation to slip inside, to rest her frozen limbs and warm her numb fingers around a cup of hot coffee, pulled at her with almost physical force. But she didn't dare.

Not when Thomas was in town searching for her.

And the longer she lingered in Walnut Springs, the more likely someone would remember seeing her. Maybe even connect her to Vincent's missing person notice.

She couldn't risk it.

A figure emerged from a building down the street, and she shrank deeper into the shadows. Just a miner by the look of him, his coat dusted with dirt or rock powder. But her heart hammered anyway, her body coiled tight and ready to run.

The miner passed without a glance in her direction, his boots crunching through the snow as he headed toward the saloon. Her pulse began to slow, but her muscles remained taut, ready to bolt.

Another man appeared, this one dressed like he lived in town, walking with purpose down the boardwalk toward her. She fumbled with the clasp on her carpetbag, ducking her head as though searching for something inside. She'd done this several times over the past hour—pretend to be occupied, avoid eye contact, wait for them to pass.

But this time, the footsteps slowed.

"Miss? Are you all right?"

She forced herself to look up. The middle-aged man stood a few feet away, concern etched across his features. His clothes marked him as a shopkeeper, maybe, or a clerk.

The kind of man who noticed things. Who remembered faces.

"I'm fine, thank you." She tried to smile, though her frozen cheeks made it hard to tell if she'd succeeded.

"You've been standing out here in the cold for quite some time." His gaze moved from her face to the carpetbag clutched against her chest. "Are you waiting for someone?"

Panic fluttered in her throat. How long had he been watching her? "Oh no, I was just—" She forced herself to take a breath, to steady the tremor in her voice. "I was just going to take a meal at the cafe."

She motioned to the building down the street, the one with the sign marking it as a boarding house and cafe. The same place she was supposed to meet James all those weeks ago, when she'd first arrived in Walnut Springs as a stranger seeking employment.

Before she'd known he was the one who posted the advertisement. His family was who she'd be working for.

The man's expression brightened with relief. "Ah, good. Mrs. Patterson serves a fine stew. You'll warm right up."

He didn't move. Just stood there watching her with that same concerned expression, waiting.

Her stomach clenched. He wasn't going to leave until she started walking. Until he'd seen her safely inside, like some misguided gentleman who'd decided she needed protecting.

She couldn't afford this attention. Couldn't risk him remembering her later, couldn't let him wonder why she'd been lurking in the shadows instead of going straight to the cafe if that had been her intention all along.

But what choice did she have?

"Thank you for your concern." The words scraped past the tightness in her throat as she forced her frozen legs to move.

Each step toward the boarding house felt like walking to her own execution. Her boots crunched through the packed snow.

Her carpetbag swung against her hip with a weight that increased with every stride.

The man remained where he was, watching. His gaze seared into her back, even after she slipped through the door of the boarding house and closed it behind her.

The warmth hit her face first, stinging her frozen cheeks until her eyes watered. She blinked against the pain and the sudden brightness, her vision adjusting to reveal a small desk tucked against the wall and a staircase directly ahead. Voices drifted from a doorway to her left—the dining room, most likely—accompanied by the clink of silverware on plates.

Her stomach twisted with the hunger she'd been ignoring for hours, but she pressed herself against the wall opposite the dining room entrance, out of sight from anyone sitting within.

That room. She would have met James there to discuss her new position, had he not come to Butte instead.

The tears surged without warning, burning hot trails down her frozen cheeks. She pressed her gloved hand to her mouth, fighting to keep the sob locked in her chest.

Leaving James had been the right thing to do. The only thing.

But she'd ripped herself in half, leaving the best part of her bleeding in that barn while the rest of her fled like the coward she'd always been.

Yet if she'd stayed… Every time he looked at her, would he remember his mother and how much he missed her? How hard it had been to grow up without her, practically an orphan, since his father lived so far away?

She couldn't bear it. Couldn't bear being the source of his pain, the constant reminder of everything he'd lost.

The voices in the dining room grew louder, footsteps approaching.

She straightened, panic jolting through her frozen limbs. She had to hide until they passed.

The staircase loomed ahead. She grabbed her carpetbag tighter and started up, her boots making soft thuds against the wooden steps. Each one felt too loud in the quiet foyer, announcing her presence to anyone around.

At the top, a narrow hallway stretched in both directions. Doors lined the walls—guest rooms, most likely. She pressed herself against the wall, straining to hear if the footsteps below had followed.

Nothing. Just the continued murmur of conversation from the dining room.

Her heart hammered against her ribs. She'd hide here until the men left the dining room, then slip back down and head straight to the livery. Buy a horse. Get out of town before anyone else tried to be helpful or asked too many questions.

Before Thomas found her.

A door opened to her right, and she glanced over.

The sight there stopped her cold, every muscle locking as panic surged once more.

The man who stepped into the hallway stopped just as suddenly, his hand still on the doorknob. His eyes widened as they locked onto hers.

Vincent Dunhill.

# CHAPTER 26

The cold bit through James's coat as Thomas pulled the wagon to a stop in front of the livery, but the chill in his gut had nothing to do with the mountain air.

He'd pushed his brothers hard to get here, the wagon rattling over frozen ruts fast enough to jar his broken leg with every bump. The laudanum had worn off an hour into the journey, leaving nothing but raw pain and sharper fear.

Robert had offered more of the bitter medicine, but James refused. He needed his mind clear, needed to think past the fog that would come with another dose.

Rose was out here somewhere. Alone. In the cold.

And Vincent could be too.

Thomas jumped down from the driver's seat and moved to help James, but he was already reaching for his walking sticks. The splint caught on the wagon's edge, sending a bolt of fire through his knee that made his vision gray at the edges. He gritted his teeth and forced himself to stand.

The livery owner stepped out to meet them, wiping his hands on his leather apron. "Evening, gentlemen. What can I do for you?"

James forced his voice to remain steady despite the way his pulse hammered against his throat. "We're looking for a woman. Red hair, green eyes. Would have come through sometime this afternoon, probably on foot."

The man's weathered face creased with thought. "Can't say I've seen anyone matching that description. Been pretty busy today."

The words twisted in his belly. She hadn't made it here yet. Either that, or she'd avoided the livery entirely, found some other way out of town. Or—

He couldn't let himself finish that thought. He couldn't envision all the possible dangers Rose might have met with.

"You're certain?" Robert's voice came from behind him.

"Pretty certain." The livery owner scratched his jaw. "Though I did step out for a spell earlier. Helped old Henderson fix a wheel on his buggy. Could've missed someone then, I suppose."

James's grip tightened on his walking sticks until the wood bit into his palms. Every second they stood here talking was another second Rose was in danger.

"We need to search the town." He turned to Thomas and Robert, ignoring the way the twist sent fresh pain lancing up his leg. "Split up. Check every building."

"Think it's better we stay together? Maybe start at Nelson's?"

James studied Thomas, trying to work through the fog of pain and exhaustion that pressed against his thoughts.

Nelson's. The saloon would be crowded this time of day— miners and ranch hands coming in from the cold, looking to warm themselves with whiskey and company. If Rose had somehow made it to town already, she wouldn't have gone there. Too many eyes. Too many questions.

But someone there might have seen her outside.

"All right." The words scraped past the tightness in his throat. "Nelson's first, then we work our way down the street."

Thomas nodded and turned to the livery owner. "Keep the horses in their harness but unhitch them from the wagon and feed them. We might need to leave in a hurry."

The three of them started toward the saloon, James's walking sticks biting into the packed, dirty snow with each step. But the physical pain was nothing compared to the fear coiling tighter around his ribs with every breath.

The saloon's weathered sign creaked above them, and lamplight spilled from the windows onto the snow-dusted boardwalk. Voices and laughter drifted through the door—the familiar sounds of men seeking warmth and company after a long day's work.

Thomas pushed through the entrance first, with Robert close behind. James followed, the sudden blast of heat and noise hitting him like an unwelcome force after the quiet cold outside.

The room stretched before him, packed with bodies and thick with the smell of whiskey, sweat, and wood smoke. His gaze swept across the crowded space, searching for any flash of auburn hair, any sign that Rose might have sought shelter here despite how unlikely it seemed.

Nothing. Just miners and ranch hands clustered around tables, their voices rising and falling in waves of conversation.

Then a familiar face emerged from the crowd near the bar. Bill Carter, the man who'd helped bring in the last of their hay before the first big snow. His weathered features were flushed with drink, and a wide grin split his face when he spotted them.

"Balfour boys!" Bill's voice boomed across the room as he worked through the crowd toward them. "Drinks are on me tonight!"

James forced his mouth into something resembling a smile, though every instinct screamed at him to push past Bill and keep searching. "That's kind of you, Bill, but we're actually—"

"Nonsense!" Bill clapped a heavy hand on James's shoulder, nearly knocking him off balance. The walking sticks slipped on the wooden floor, and Robert's hand shot out to steady him. "You boys worked hard on that hay. Let me show my appreciation."

The stench of whiskey rolled off Bill, and his eyes held that glassy brightness that came with being several drinks past sober. The smell grew even worse when he leaned in. "'Sides, got me a windfall today. Biggest payday I've seen in years."

The words slid ice down James's spine. A windfall. A big payday. Like the fifty-dollar reward Vincent offered for information about Rose?

He tightened his grip on the walking sticks, fighting to keep his expression neutral despite the sick dread pooling in his gut. "That so? What kind of windfall?"

Bill's eyes went unfocused a moment, then he shook his head with exaggerated care. "Oh, you know. Just some work that paid better than expected."

"What kind of work?" Robert's voice came out casual, but James heard the edge beneath it.

"This and that." Bill waved a wild hand toward the bar, nearly taking out the man passing by behind him. "Come on, let me buy you boys a drink. Nelson's got some decent whiskey in tonight."

James tightened his jaw. Every second spent playing games with this drunk ranch hand was another second Rose remained in danger. But pushing too hard might make Bill suspicious, might make him clam up entirely if he did know something.

"Appreciate the offer, Bill." He shifted his weight on the walking sticks, trying to ease the pressure on his throbbing leg. "But we're actually looking for someone. A woman with red hair, green eyes. She might have come through town this afternoon."

Bill's expression didn't change, but something flicked in his unfocused gaze—too quick to read, gone so quick, it might not have actually been there.

"Red hair, you say?" Bill scratched his whiskered jaw, swaying a little. "Can't say I've seen anyone like that. Then again, been in here since—" He paused, squinting as though trying to remember. "Since noon, maybe? Time gets away from a man when Nelson's pouring generous."

The words should have brought relief. If Bill had been drinking since noon, he couldn't have been the one to spot Rose and turn her in to Vincent. But the sick feeling in James's gut only intensified. Someone else could have seen her. Could have recognized her from Vincent's description and collected that reward.

"You know a man named Vincent Dunhill?" Robert's question cut through the noise of the saloon.

Bill blinked, and his gaze shifted between the three of them. "Who?"

"Dunhill." Robert moved closer, his voice dropping low enough that the surrounding noise wouldn't cover their conversation. "City fellow. Maybe asking questions around town."

Bill's brow furrowed, his alcohol-fogged mind clearly struggling to process the description. He swayed again, catching himself against a nearby table. "Dunhill? That a first name or last?"

"Last name." James forced the words past the tightness in his throat. "Vincent Dunhill. Tall fellow, well-dressed. Looks like he's from back east."

Recognition didn't dawn on Bill's face. The man just shook his head, his movements exaggerated and sloppy. "Nope. Don't know no Dunhill."

"He the fellow who looks like he's from the big city and thinks too highly of himself?" A voice cut through from somewhere behind them.

James turned to the speaker, his leg screaming in protest. A lean man in miner's clothes sat at a poker table behind them, a half-empty glass in his hand. "I passed him riding out of town an hour ago."

The words twisted inside him. Vincent had been here. In Walnut Springs. And now he was gone.

With Rose?

The thought sent panic clawing up his throat. "Which direction was he headed?"

"Northwest, I think. Toward that main pass that goes to the Mullan road." The miner scratched his jaw, his eyes narrowing in thought.

"Did he have anyone with him?" James had to hold himself back from gripping the man's shirt and hauling the answers out of him. "The man you saw. Was he alone?"

The miner's brow furrowed. "Looked to be alone, far as I could tell. Though I only saw him for a minute or two when our paths crossed on the trail."

Alone. Vincent had been alone when he'd left town.

Relief flooded through him. If Vincent had found Rose, he would have her with him. Unless—

Unless Vincent had stashed her somewhere. Left her tied up while he rode ahead to…what? Scout the route? Make arrangements?

James's pulse hammered as the possibilities splintered through his mind, each one worse than the last.

"Did you notice if he stopped anywhere in town?" Thomas stepped closer to the miner. "Maybe went into any buildings?"

The miner shook his head. "Like I said, I only saw him for a minute on the trail. Didn't see him in town at all."

Dead end. The information twisted in James's gut, useless and frustrating. Vincent had been here, had left, and they still had no idea where Rose was.

"We need to check the buildings." James turned toward the door, his walking sticks already moving. Every second they wasted standing here was another second Rose could be in danger.

Robert's hand closed around his arm, stopping him. "James, think this through. If Vincent left an hour ago heading northwest, and Rose hasn't shown up at the livery…"

The unspoken possibility hung between them. Rose might have never reached town. Maybe she avoided Walnut Springs entirely, taking some other route. Or Vincent might have found her before she ever made it this far.

His chest constricted until breathing felt like dragging air through mud. "We have to go after him. We have to know for sure whether it's Vincent, and if he has Rose."

He didn't waste time with more words, just spun and hobbled through the door to the icy darkness outside.

# CHAPTER 27

Rose's head pounded with a vicious ache that made her stomach roil. Pain pulsed behind her eyes in waves that matched the jarring motion beneath her.

Motion?

Her thoughts moved like honey in winter, thick and slow, refusing to connect properly. Cold bit through her clothes—deeper than the mountain air should feel, seeping into her bones until her whole body shook with it. And that smell. Chemical and bitter, coating the inside of her mouth and nose until every breath tasted wrong.

She tried to move, but her arms wouldn't respond. Her legs felt distant, heavy, like they belonged to someone else entirely. The darkness behind her eyelids pressed down with weight, and forcing them open took more effort than climbing a mountain.

The world tilted sideways.

No...she was sideways.

Draped over something hard that dug into her ribs with each jarring step. A saddle. She was draped over a saddle, face down, the leather grinding into her ribs as the horse beneath her plodded forward.

Memories eased in through her foggy mind.

The boarding house. The hallway. Vincent's face appearing in the doorway, his cold eyes widening with recognition and triumph. She'd tried to run, tried to scream, but he'd been too quick.

He grabbed her and clamped his hand over her mouth before sound could escape. The struggle became brief and futile. Especially when he pressed a cloth against her face. That awful chemical smell filled her lungs as the world dissolved into darkness.

He must have given her something to force sleep.

The horse beneath her halted and relief eased through her aching middle. But then rough hands grabbed her waist, hauling her down. Her legs buckled when they touched ground, and she would have collapsed if Vincent's grip hadn't tightened, holding her upright with harsh force.

"Careful now." His voice cut through the ringing in her ears, cold and conversational, like they were discussing the weather instead of her kidnapping. "You'll hurt yourself if you fall."

She tried to speak, tried to scream, but her throat was raw and her tongue felt thick and useless. The sound that escaped was barely a whimper.

"None of that." Vincent's fingers dug into her arms as he dragged her forward. "Save your voice. You'll need it soon enough."

The world tilted and swayed with each forced step. Her boots scraped against frozen ground, then wood—a porch, maybe? The details wouldn't come into focus. Everything blurred at the edges, her focus slipping away every time she tried to grasp it.

A door creaked open. The smell hit her first—rotten wood and animal droppings mixed with something older, deeper—the stench of abandonment. A building left empty too long.

Vincent kicked something aside, and the scrape of wood

against wood echoed in the enclosed space. Then he shoved her, and she stumbled forward, her knees hitting what felt like a chair. The impact sent fresh waves of nausea churning through her stomach.

"Sit." His hand pressed down on her shoulder, forcing her onto the seat. The wood creaked beneath her weight, unsteady, like it might collapse at any moment.

She tried to focus on his face, but the features kept swimming in and out of clarity. Just the sharp line of his jaw. The cold calculation in his eyes. That awful smile playing at the corners of his mouth.

"There now." He brushed snow from his expensive coat with the same fastidious care he'd always shown for his appearance. "Not quite what I'm accustomed to, but it will do for the night. By tomorrow, we'll be far enough away we can travel more comfortably."

The words penetrated slowly through the fog still clinging to her thoughts. Tomorrow. Travel. Away.

He was taking her somewhere. Back to Virginia City, probably. Back to that stage where drunk men leered and grabbed, where Vincent controlled every breath she took, every word she spoke.

Back to that contract.

Terror burned through the chemical haze, sharp enough to cut. She tried to push herself up from the chair, but her arms trembled and gave out under her weight. She slumped back, her vision blurring once more.

Rope appeared in Vincent's hands—where had he gotten rope?—and he reached for her wrists. The sight flared another spike of panic through her chest, but her body refused to respond. Her muscles felt disconnected, useless, like they'd forgotten how to obey her commands.

"Now, now." His fingers closed around her left wrist, cold

even through her glove. "Don't make this harder than it needs to be."

She tried to pull away, but the movement was weak. Pathetic. He easily captured her other wrist and drew both arms behind the chair. The rope bit into her skin as he wrapped it around and around, securing her to the chair back with a powerful tug.

When he finished, he stepped back to examine his work, brushing dust from his hands like he'd just completed some mundane household task. "Much better. Can't have you wandering off in the night, can we?"

She forced her eyes to focus on his face, fighting against the pull of whatever clouded her thoughts. She held his gaze. Did her best to let him see that she wasn't broken yet, no matter what he'd done.

His smile widened, sharp and cold as a knife blade. "Still have some fight left in you I see. Good. The audiences prefer a performance with spirit." He moved toward what looked like a rusty stove in the corner. "Though I must say, you've caused me considerable trouble. Running off like that. Making me chase you all the way to this godforsaken wilderness."

Her throat ached with the need to speak, to scream, to tell him exactly what she thought of him and his theater and his cursed contract. But the words wouldn't form properly. Her tongue was too thick and clumsy, and the few sounds she managed came out as weak rasps that barely carried across the small space.

"Save your strength." Vincent knelt beside the stove, examining it with a critical eye. "You'll need your voice in top condition soon enough. Though I suppose a few days of rest won't hurt. Give that pretty throat of yours time to recover from all that screaming you did before I could properly sedate you."

The memory flickered through the haze—the boarding house hallway, his hand clamping over her mouth, her muffled cries against his palm before that awful cloth pressed against her face. Had anyone heard her? Would anyone come looking?

James.

If only she'd never left the ranch. Never ran from the hard task of facing the past. Maybe James could still care for her given time.

But wishing changed nothing. She was here now, bound to this chair in a rotting cabin while Vincent prepared to drag her back into captivity.

# CHAPTER 28

$\mathcal{W}$ith every jolt of the wagon, James welcomed the pain.

It kept him sharp, kept the panic from swallowing him whole every time his mind conjured images of Rose in Vincent's hands. He gripped the reins tighter, urging the team faster down the dark, rutted trail.

Somewhere ahead, Thomas and Robert rode horses borrowed from the livery, eating up the miles faster than this rumbling wagon could manage.

He'd sent them on because it made sense, because they could cover more ground, because a man with a broken leg had no business trying to ride astride through mountain wilderness in the dark. He'd already learned that lesson once.

But logic did nothing to ease the burning need to be the one who found her. To be the one who protected her.

To make up for standing in that barn like one of the support beams while she'd apologized for sins that weren't hers to carry.

The well-traveled main trail stretched ahead in the moonlight, winding between snow-heavy pines that pressed close on either side. He scanned the darkness for any sign of his brothers returning, for any movement that might signal they'd caught up to Vincent.

Unless Vincent had turned off somewhere.

The thought made his chest tighten so hard he could barely breathe. Vincent could have taken any number of side trails branching off this main route—paths that wound deeper into the wilderness, leading to abandoned mining camps or forgotten homesteads where no one would hear a woman scream.

He forced the images away before they could take root. Vincent might not even have Rose at all.

All James could do was keep going and use every one of his senses to find clues. Anything that might lead him to her.

As the wagon rounded a cluster of boulders in the trail, he caught it—faint wood smoke on the icy breeze. He pulled the team to a stop and sat perfectly still, testing the wind. Not just his imagination. Definitely smoke. In the dark sky, he couldn't see any sign of which direction it might be coming from.

He glanced at the ground, straining to decipher the shadows in the snow. Were those tracks? Or just uneven ground beneath the layer of white?

They had to be tracks. The ice crystals looked churned in some places. And there seemed to be a straight line of them. A single animal, maybe a horse.

He lifted his focus to the trees and shrubs his team would have to travel through to follow the tracks. The trees were spaced far enough apart, the wagon might actually be able to fit. Perhaps this had once been a road.

The scent of smoke had grown stronger. He had to find out for sure whether or not Vincent went this way. There weren't enough tracks for his brothers to have searched this route. They'd likely been moving too fast to see a single set of prints veer off or smell the smoke.

He guided the team off the main trail, the horses stepping

higher through the new snow and the wagon lurching more over the uneven ground.

The tracks became clearer as they progressed—definitely a single horse, recently passed. The prints cut through the snow in a line too straight to be from a wandering animal. Someone had ridden this way with purpose.

Every step brought the scent thicker, cutting through the crisp mountain air with the unmistakable tang of burning wood.

The trail—if it could be called that—narrowed as the trees pressed closer. Branches scraped against the wagon's sides, and twice he had to guide the team around fallen logs half-buried in snow.

The path was too rough now, too overgrown. He couldn't risk breaking an axle or getting stuck.

He pulled the horses to a halt and sat listening. The forest pressed in around him, silent except for the wind sifting through pine needles and the creak of snow-laden branches. No voices. No sound of movement.

But that smoke meant someone was out here.

He set the brake and wrapped the reins around the brake handle, then reached for his walking sticks and the rifle from the bench beside him. He couldn't manage both at once, but he didn't dare proceed without a weapon. Hopefully, he could hold the gun in the same hand as one of the walking sticks.

His boots hit the snow, and the splint jammed into his flesh as his full weight came down on it. Sweat dampened his back despite the cold.

He sucked in a breath, though, and pressed forward. The snow covered his boots, dampening his trousers and forcing him to drag his splinted leg behind him.

Finally, the trees thinned ahead, revealing a dark shape against the snow—a structure of some kind, small and hunched. An old trapper's cabin maybe, long since abandoned.

But smoke curled from a rusted stovepipe jutting through the roof, and a single horse stood tied to a post near the entrance.

His pulse hammered against his throat. Someone was definitely inside.

Vincent? Or just a traveler seeking shelter from the cold?

He edged closer, using the trees for cover. The horse lifted its head, and James tensed. *Don't nicker. Don't make a sound.*

Surprise might be his only advantage. That and his rifle.

Before he could make a plan, though, he had to know for sure who was inside that cabin.

# CHAPTER 29

The stench of decay was almost worse than the numbing cold.

Rose forced her lungs to expand slowly, fighting the nausea that still churned in her middle from whatever Vincent had used to drug her earlier. The chemical taste coated her tongue, mixing with the stench of animal droppings that littered the corners of this wretched cabin. Moonlight filtered through holes in the roof and walls, creating pale pools on the filthy floor that did nothing to warm the space.

She kept her breathing slow and even, her gaze fixed on the feet in front of her while she watched him from the edges of her vision.

Small. Invisible. That's what she needed to be right now. The old survival instinct—learned through years of living under his control—urged her to fade into the background, to become so quiet and unobtrusive he might forget she existed.

She hated that instinct. Hated the way it still rose up so automatically. But it was the safest way to be around Vincent.

The rope bit into her wrists where he'd tied her to the

broken chair. At least he'd left her feet free—a mistake on his part, maybe, or simple arrogance. He'd always been stronger than her in many ways, but she didn't have to let that remain true forever. She had strength of mind and determination.

The chair creaked beneath her with every tiny shift of weight, the wood so rotted it felt like it might collapse at any moment.

The tin stove in the center of the room worked, surprisingly enough. Vincent had coaxed a small fire to life inside it, though the warmth it threw barely reached her.

Vincent crouched before the stove, feeding another piece of wood into the flames. The firelight caught the silver in his hair, making him look distinguished even in this hovel.

He'd always been like that—able to maintain his veneer of cultured elegance no matter the circumstances. As though the rot inside him couldn't quite penetrate the carefully constructed exterior.

He stood and pulled a glass bottle from his coat pocket, then a cloth. A sickly-sweet smell drifted through the air, and her insides lurched with recognition. That had to be what he'd used to make her sleep in the boarding house.

He turned to her with that awful, familiar smile. "I really hoped you'd be more reasonable." He uncorked the bottle and doused the cloth, holding it at arm's length. "We could have had a pleasant journey back to Virginia City. But you've always had to make things difficult, haven't you? Just like your mother."

The mention of Mama spiked a surge of fury through her fear. Her mother had been trapped, manipulated, forced into choices no woman should have to make. And Vincent spoke of her like *she'd* been the problem.

He approached her, the sweet-smelling cloth held casually in his hand, his confidence absolute. He thought she was still that frightened fifteen-year-old girl who'd signed her life away. He thought she was broken.

But she wasn't broken. She was angry.

When he reached out to press the cloth over her face, she slammed her boots into his groin with every ounce of strength she could muster.

Vincent staggered back, gasping, and Rose lunged to her feet. The chair came with her—still tied to her upper body, forcing her to bend forward. But the broken wood was lighter than she'd expected, and she could move.

He recovered faster than she'd hoped. His hand shot out, catching her shoulder, but she spun away. The chair swung with her, its legs catching him in the ribs with a satisfying crack.

He cursed and came at her again. She thrust backward into him, plunging the chair legs like a weapon.

He stumbled into the stove, his hand shooting out to catch himself. The metal rang with the impact, and he hissed through his teeth.

They struggled in the cramped space—he was stronger, always had been—but she was fighting for survival now, for her future. For the right to choose James and the ranch and the life she craved with everything in her.

She swung the chair wildly, screaming with everything she had, just in case someone—anyone—was close enough to hear.

Vincent's fist connected with the side of her face near her jaw, snapping her head sideways. Stars burst behind her eyes, and her knees buckled, but she couldn't give up.

His fingers closed around her throat, squeezing, cutting off the scream still clawing its way from her chest. The cabin tilted sideways, darkness creeping in at the edges of her vision. Her lungs burned. She thrashed against him, but his grip only tightened.

Black spots danced across her vision. Her lungs pleaded for air.

*God, help me!*

The words weren't eloquent. They were barely even words—

more a soul-deep cry torn from the last fragment of her consciousness.

The door exploded inward.

God must have heard.

# CHAPTER 30

Ice and fire merged in James's veins at the sight of Vincent's hands around Rose's throat.

He raised the rifle to his shoulder, his grip steady despite the white-hot fury coursing through his veins.

He couldn't shoot Vincent outright, not with Rose in front of the man and struggling. But he had to stop the beast from choking her

"Let her go." His voice cut through the sounds of struggle—Rose's choked gasps, Vincent's labored breathing.

Vincent froze. His hand remained wrapped around Rose's throat, but his body went rigid as he turned to face James in the doorway. For one heartbeat, no one moved.

Then Vincent's face twisted into something ugly—fear and calculation warring for dominance. He yanked Rose tighter in front of him like a shield, one hand still gripping her throat. "You won't shoot." The words came out tight, strained. "You'll hit her."

James's finger trembled on the trigger. The rifle sight wavered, and every instinct screamed at him to pull, to end this, to make Vincent pay for every bruise on Rose's face, every mark his fingers left on her throat. Every scar his dominance and lies had left on her heart.

But Vincent was right.

In the dim firelight, with Rose struggling in his grip, the risk was too great. One inch off, and he could kill the woman he loved.

"Put it down, Balfour. Put it down, or I swear I'll snap her neck right here."

James's mind raced through options, each one worse than the last. His splinted leg made it impossible to lunge for a better angle. He could wait Vincent out, but the man was desperate now. Cornered. And desperate men did awful things.

Rose's eyes met his across the cabin, wide with fear but also with something else—trust. She trusted him to save her. The rifle felt like lead in his hands, useless despite its power.

The one thing he couldn't risk was Rose's life.

"All right." James lowered the weapon and leaned it against the wall.

Vincent's expression relaxed—just a fraction, but enough.

Rose must have felt it. Her heel drove into Vincent's knee. He stumbled backward, his arm releasing her throat. She threw herself forward, away from him.

James lunged.

He had to get to Rose. To get between her and Vincent.

Vincent recovered and charged forward. James met his blow with his shoulder, shoving back. They melded into a tangle of limbs, then crashed into the cabin's rickety table. It collapsed beneath their weight in a shower of splinters.

Vincent possessed the advantage of not being injured, but James had desperation and fury on his side. Vincent's fist connected with James's jaw, snapping his head back, but James didn't let go. He drove Vincent backward into the wall, and the entire structure shuddered.

They grappled on the filthy floor, James's broken leg twisted. Bolts of white-hot agony shot through his body. But the pain only fueled his rage.

This man had tried to drag Rose back into slavery, and James would die before he let that happen.

Vincent rolled on top of him, his hands closing around James's throat. He fought for breath, his hands gripping the knave's shoulders. Vincent's arms were longer though, giving him—

The pressure built, darkness creeping in at the edges of his vision. His lungs burned.

Rose appeared behind Vincent, a cloth in her hand. She'd somehow worked one of her arms out of the ropes that bound her to the chair. She pressed the rag to Vincent's snarling open mouth.

The surprise made his grip on James's throat loosen, just enough for him to suck in a desperate gulp of air.

Vincent jerked his head away from the rag, but whatever that sweet fragrance was must have already started to work. His movements slowed, turning clumsy. The iron fingers around James's neck weakened.

James shoved hard, throwing the villain off balance. He toppled sideways, and James rolled with him, ignoring the agony from his broken leg.

He had to pin Vincent down. Had to keep him there so Rose—

She crouched beside James and pressed the cloth again to Vincent's face with her free hand. Ropes still bound her body and other arm to the splintered chair pieces.

Vincent thrashed beneath them, weaker now, his struggles growing sluggish. At last, his eyes rolled back, unfocused.

His body went slack.

James couldn't trust it. He kept the weight of his good knee pressed down on Vincent's chest, his hands pinning the man's shoulders to the grimy floor.

His own chest heaved, dragging in air that tasted like rot and chemicals and blood. The room tilted sideways, and he blinked hard to clear his vision.

"Is he…" Rose's voice came out hoarse, raw from whatever this blackguard had done to her.

"Out." James forced the word through his own burning throat. "For now."

He didn't move. Couldn't make himself ease the pressure keeping Vincent pinned. The security of Vincent's body beneath him felt like the only solid thing in a world gone sideways.

Rose's hand trembled against his shoulder. "James, you can let go now."

Could he? Every muscle in his body screamed to hold on, to make sure this monster couldn't rise again.

The chemical sweetness of whatever Rose had used still hung in the air, coating the back of his throat and mixing with the copper taste of blood in his mouth.

His broken leg had twisted beneath him at some point during the fight—he couldn't remember when exactly, only that each breath sent fresh waves of fire shooting from knee to hip. The splint dug into his flesh through his torn trousers, and warmth trickled down his calf that could be either blood or sweat. He couldn't tell anymore.

"Jamie." Rose's voice cracked on his name. "Please."

Her words finally broke through the red haze clouding his vision. He forced his fingers to loosen, one by one.

Rose had laid the cloth over Vincent's mouth and nose, and the man's chest continued its shallow rise and fall beneath him —unconscious, not dead.

James finally rolled off Vincent's chest, his broken leg screaming as he turned. The room spun, and he had to brace one hand against the grubby floor to keep from pitching sideways.

But Rose needed him. He had to keep his senses about him.

She knelt beside him, still bound to the splintered chair back, her hair wild from all the fighting. Bruises darkened her throat in the shape of Vincent's fingers, and her face—her beautiful face—showed a purple bloom on her right cheek where that monster must have struck her.

She started to wiggle out of the ropes, and he helped work the chair out from behind her. Once she pushed the ropes down the length of her skirt and off her feet, she turned to him.

He didn't wait. Couldn't wait.

He pulled her into his arms, ignoring the way his leg twisted beneath him, ignoring the fire that shot through every nerve ending.

Nothing mattered except the solid weight of her in his arms, the proof that she was alive, that he'd reached her in time.

God had protected her. Protected them both.

She collapsed into him, her body shaking so fierce, he could feel it in his bones. Her fingers seized his coat, clutching the fabric like he might disappear if she loosened her grip.

Never. He would never leave her side again if he had any say-so in the matter.

The trembling in her body worked its way into his own chest, settling there alongside the terror that still hadn't quite released its hold on his ribs.

"I'm sorry." His throat still burned from Vincent's chokehold, making his voice raw. "Rose, I'm so sorry. For the barn, for standing there useless when you needed me to tell you—" His words cracked, and he had to force the rest out past the tightness. "For letting you believe even for a second that I blamed you or your mother for what that monster did."

"I know." Tears spilled down her cheeks, cutting clean tracks through the grime coating her skin. "Jamie, I know. I should never have run. I should have trusted you."

The way she said his name—the childhood nickname only she had ever used—broke something loose in his chest. He pulled her closer, burying his face in her hair and breathing in the scent of her.

She was real. Solid. Alive.

And safe.

# CHAPTER 31

The rope burned against Rose's fingers as she pulled it tight around Vincent's wrists.

His body slumped against the cabin's central support post, dead weight that would have toppled sideways if not for the beam at his back. The chloroform had done its work—his chest rose and fell in shallow breaths, his face slack from unconsciousness.

But Rose didn't trust it. Didn't trust him.

She wrapped another loop around his wrists, then another around his entire body. Her hands wouldn't stop shaking, making the simple task so much harder. Every muscle in her body screamed for rest, but she couldn't stop moving.

She couldn't let herself think about what might have happened if James hadn't found her. If he'd arrived even minutes later. Only God could bring rescue at that exact moment she'd needed it most.

The moment she'd finally trusted the fight into God's hands.

"That's good." James's voice came from somewhere behind her, rough and strained. "He's not going anywhere."

She forced herself to tie off the knot, making a double—no a triple knot, then stepped back and studied her work.

"He's not going anywhere." James repeated the words, but this time his voice dragged.

She glanced over at him, slumped against the cabin wall where he'd collapsed after helping her drag Vincent to the post. His face had gone gray beneath the grime and blood, his breathing labored. The splint on his leg had broken, and it was impossible to tell how much damage had been done to the bone beneath. Dark stains spread across his trouser leg that she desperately hoped were mud and not blood.

James. Her heart swelled with so much love for this man, she might not be able to contain it all.

She'd spent years convincing herself she didn't deserve this—that no man would love her enough to set aside his own happiness for hers. That she didn't deserve a man who would risk everything to save her, who would break himself trying to reach her in time. Who would look at her not with blame or disgust, but with a love so fierce it broke down every one of her defenses.

"We need to get you warm." She moved toward him and lowered to her knees at his side. "And that leg—"

"I'm fine." The words came out rough. Unconvincing.

He wasn't fine. Not even close. But arguing with him would waste precious energy neither of them had to spare.

His eyes met hers, green and clear despite the pain etched into every line of his face. The way he looked at her—like she was something precious, something worth loving—made tears blur her vision.

"How did you find me?"

He shifted against the wall, grimacing with the movement. "As soon as we realized you were gone, Robert, Thomas, and I went after you."

Her heart clenched at the thought of all three brothers

charging after her through the cold, snowy wilderness. "You shouldn't have come. Not with your leg—"

"Don't." His voice came out sharp enough to make her flinch. He softened his tone immediately. "Don't tell me I shouldn't have come for you. There's nowhere you could go that I wouldn't follow."

The comfort of those words settled into her chest, warm and solid despite the bitter cold around them. She reached for his hand, her fingers still trembling as they closed around his.

His palm was ice against hers. Was he not wearing gloves? Actually, neither of them were. When had she lost hers? During the struggle with Vincent? She couldn't remember.

"We need to get you warmer." She looked around the wretched cabin, cataloging what little resources they had. The fire in the tin stove still burned, throwing weak light and weaker heat into the frigid space.

"There are blankets in the wagon. We should fire a shot, too, to signal my brothers if they're still close enough to hear."

"I'll take care of it." She pushed herself to her feet, her legs protesting the movement. Every muscle felt bruised and battered from the struggle with Vincent, and her throat still ached where his fingers had squeezed.

She scooped up the rifle where it still leaned against the wall by the door. Her fingers closed around the metal, the feel of it awkward in her grip. She'd never fired a gun before—never had the chance to learn with Vincent's endless smothering—but she couldn't tell James that. Not when determination had replaced some of the gray pallor in his face.

"Fire twice in the air away from the cabin."

"Two shots." She nodded and turned toward the door, forcing her feet to carry her back into the frigid night.

She managed to fire the rifle, though her ears still rang from the blasts and her shoulder ached from the way the gun slammed back into her.

It wasn't hard to find the wagon and retrieve the blankets. The horses seemed safe enough still hitched to the wagon. Not comfortable perhaps, but not in danger or pain. She had no warm barn or mound of hay to feed them. They all just needed to settle in and wait—until Robert and Thomas came...until morning...she had no idea what would come first.

James opened weary, pain-filled eyes when she sank down beside him again.

Seeing him like this made her own eyes sting. "Is there anything I can do to ease the pain? Maybe...would a whiff of that chloroform help?" Though her insides twisted at the thought of being left alone here if Vincent woke while James lay in a drugged sleep.

He kept his head resting back against the wall, but rolled it side to side. "Just sit with me so we can both get warm."

His best idea yet. She scanned the room once more to make sure she didn't need to attend to anything else before settling in for the night. The fire was stoked, and Vincent still slept where he was tied.

She settled in beside James, spreading one blanket over their legs and the other covering their upper bodies. He slipped an arm behind her, pulling her close to him.

She turned in so she could rest her head on his shoulder. He wrapped both arms around her, tucking her as close as their bodies would allow. Her forehead pressed into the curve of his neck, her breath warming the small space between them. Little by little, his warmth, the security of being held in his arms...

She'd never felt so safe—so loved—in her entire life.

Even the bitter wind seeping through the cabin walls couldn't touch the heat spreading through her chest as James held her like he would never let her go.

His heartbeat thrummed steady against her ear—a little too fast perhaps, but strong. Real.

She closed her eyes. Let herself settle, sinking deeper into his embrace. Let the rhythm of their breathing flow together. The rough wool of his coat scratched her cheek—a reminder that this was real, that she was here, pressed close.

His scent closed around her, sweat and leather, and beneath that, something richer, something purely his. Not new to her but woven into her earliest memories. The best memories.

A scent that spoke of adventure. Not the kind that frightened. The kind that promised possibility. She let herself feel it, all of it, letting the comfort and excitement and memory wrap around her as surely as his arms did.

They should talk about what happened.

Talk about the letter even, and what Vincent had done to his mother. She should explain why she'd run. Apologize. But the words tangled in her throat, knotted together with exhaustion and fear and this warmth that felt so much like home.

Finally she forced herself to speak. "I thought you'd hate me." The words slipped out barely more than a whisper against his chest. "When I told you about Vincent and your mother—the way you just stood there, not saying anything, I was certain you blamed me."

His arms tightened around her, and his voice rumbled through his chest before the words reached her ears. "I could never hate you. Never." His chest lifted in a sigh. "I was in shock. Trying to process that my mother might have been murdered, that Vincent had done it. But not once—not for a single second —did I think it was your fault or your mother's."

The tears came then, hot and fast, raging past her defenses and spilling down her cheeks. Years of carrying guilt for what Vincent had done—the power of it crashing over her until she could barely breathe. But James's arms remained steady around her, anchoring her through the storm.

James's hand moved to her hair, his fingers tangling in the matted strands. "It's all right. You're safe now."

But it wasn't just about being safe. It was about being seen—

truly seen—and still being loved. Still being wanted despite everything Vincent had twisted and broken inside her.

"I should have stayed." The words came out thick, choking her. "Should have trusted you to—"

"You were protecting yourself." His voice held no accusation, only understanding that made her chest ache. "After everything Vincent put you through, of course you ran when you thought I might turn you away. When I stood there like a rock instead of telling you what you needed to hear."

She pulled back, just enough to look up at his face. The firelight from the stove caught the planes of his features, throwing shadows across the bruises already forming on his jaw. "What did I need to hear?"

His green eyes held hers, clear and steady despite the pain that must be tearing through his broken leg. "That I love you. That nothing Vincent did, nothing your mother did or didn't do —not even anything you could do—would ever change how I feel about you."

His hand rose to cup her face. His thumb brushed across her aching cheekbone with a gentleness that spilled fresh tears down her face. "You're the strongest, bravest woman I've ever known. I want to spend the rest of my life proving to you how much you're worth loving."

The words poured into her heart, filling spaces she hadn't realized were empty until this moment. She'd spent so long believing Vincent's lies—that she was nothing without him, that no one would want her once they knew the truth of what she'd been.

But James looked at her like she hung the stars, like her scars made her beautiful instead of broken.

"I love you too." The words rose from the deepest parts of her. "I think I always have. Even when we were children."

A smile crept over his battered face, brightening his gray exhaustion. "Then marry me. Not because you need rescuing or because you have nowhere else to go. Because you want to build a life with me. Because you choose this—choose us."

Marriage. A real life with James.

Not as his employee or his ward, but as his wife. His partner.

She searched his face, scanning for any hint of doubt or obligation. The only emotions there were warmth. Certainty. Love so fierce her tears started to well again. How could this man be so good? And how could he possibly be hers? Only God could give her a gift this overwhelming. Broken years could not be returned—but maybe they could be redeemed.

"Yes." She could only whisper the word. So much love, so many years of longing. Finally finding their home in him. "I would love to marry you."

His smile overwhelmed even the pain creasing beneath his eyes, and he pulled her closer.

His lips found hers. So gentle. A caress that wove all the way to her soul. A hint of blood flavored this kiss—his or hers, she couldn't tell—but it didn't matter.

Nothing mattered except this moment, this promise, this man who'd broken himself trying to reach her. And the God Who'd brought them back together.

# CHAPTER 32

The sound of hoofbeats pulled James from the edges of sleep where he'd been drifting, his body pressed close to Rose's warmth beneath the scratchy wool blankets in this freezing old cabin.

He forced his eyes open, though every muscle in his body screamed to stay exactly where he was—Rose warm against his chest, her breathing steady and even in sleep.

But those hoofbeats meant rescue—hopefully. Meant getting Rose somewhere safe, reaching help for his leg that had swollen to twice its normal size during the night. Would Doc Morrison still be at the ranch helping Mandie with the birth?

Probably. It was hard to believe all of that had started less than a day ago. His life had changed in these last twenty-four hours.

For the better. Definitely for the better.

Voices sounded outside. Thomas's raised shout cutting through the pre-dawn stillness, then Robert's lower reply. Hopefully his brothers would realize the two shots together meant they were safe.

His brothers had found them.

He shifted carefully, trying not to wake Rose, but she stirred anyway. Her eyes fluttered open, confusion clouding them for a heartbeat before awareness settled.

"It's all right." He kept his voice low, though the effort scraped against his raw throat. "My brothers are here."

She pushed herself upright, and the blanket fell away from her shoulders. The bruises on her throat looked darker in the gray morning light filtering through the gaps in the cabin's walls. A new round of anger twisted beneath his ribs at the sight.

Vincent still slumped against the post where they'd tied him, his head lolled forward. The chloroform had worn off hours ago —James had heard the change in his breathing around midnight —but the ropes held.

Boot steps crunched through snow outside, approaching the cabin door.

"James!" Thomas's voice cut through the morning quiet. "You in there?"

"We're here. Rose is safe."

The door burst open, and Thomas filled the doorway, concern masking his face. It shifted to relief the moment his eyes landed on them.

Robert stepped behind him, his expression harder to read but no less relieved.

Thomas's gaze swept the cabin—taking in Vincent tied to the post, the broken splint on James's leg, the bruises marking Rose's face and throat. His jaw tightened, a muscle jumping beneath his skin.

"We heard the shots last night and came back, but didn't see where the wagon turned off until dawn." Robert moved past Thomas, his eyes logging every detail of the room.

James tried to push himself up, but his leg refused to cooperate. The swelling had made the limb feel like it belonged to someone else entirely—hot and tight and pulsing with every heartbeat. "Vincent drugged Rose to make her sleep. Tried to take her back to Virginia City."

Thomas's expression turned cold in a way James had rarely seen from his youngest brother. He crossed to where Vincent slumped against the post and nudged him with his boot—not gently. "Still out?"

"No." He had to clear his raw throat to make the words come out loud enough. "He woke hours ago. Just hasn't moved much."

As if on cue, Vincent's head lifted. His gray eyes—clearer now than they'd been last night—swept the cabin before settling on James with a look that slid down his spine.

No fear there. No remorse. Just cold calculation, like he was already planning his next move.

"Gentlemen." Vincent's voice came out smooth despite the circumstances, that cultured eastern accent perfectly intact. "I believe there's been a misunderstanding."

James's fingers curled against the rough wool blanket. That voice—smooth as silk, reasonable as a judge—was the same one that had charmed Rose's mother years ago. The same one that had twisted contracts and threats into chains.

Thomas's hand went to the knife at his belt. "The only misunderstanding here is you thinking you'd get away with this."

Vincent's mouth curved into something that might have been a smile on a different face. On his, it looked like a blade. "I have a contract. Legally binding. Miss Prescott is obligated to fulfill the terms of her employment, and I was merely—"

"Save it for the law." Robert's voice cut through Vincent's words like a sharp ax through rotten wood. "You're going to answer for what you did to Miss Prescott, to her mother, and to our own mother."

Vincent didn't respond, just glared at the two men standing over him. Robert's focus shifted from Vincent to James, his gaze sweeping over the blanket, though he probably couldn't see anything. "Can you ride in the wagon back to town? We need to get you to the doc, but he's probably still at the ranch with Mandie."

"Mandie?" Rose straightened beside him.

James shifted his hand to find hers beneath the blanket. "The baby started coming yesterday morning. That's why it took us so long to realize you'd left. I had to ride out to fetch my brothers from the high pasture."

She wove her fingers between his. "Then we should get back as soon as possible. She'll want help."

If he weren't hurting so bad, he might have chuckled at her need to care for others, even after what she'd been through.

He squeezed her hand. "We will."

Robert moved closer, crouching to lift the blanket from James's extended legs. His brother's expression tightened as his gaze traveled from knee to ankle, taking in the torn splint and the dark stains that probably weren't sweat.

The scrutiny made him want to pull away, to insist he was fine, but the swelling spoke for itself.

"This needs proper attention." Robert straightened, his jaw set with that Balfour determination. "Thomas, help me get him to the wagon. We'll tie Vincent to his horse and lead him back."

The next few minutes blurred in waves of pain. His brothers lifted him—careful as they could be—but every movement sent fire shooting through the broken bone.

Rose hovered close, holding his splinted leg steady as Thomas and Robert maneuvered him through the cabin door and into the pale morning light.

The cold air bit at his face, sharp enough to clear some of the fog from his head.

The wagon sat where he'd left it, the horses blowing clouds of steam in the frigid air.

After the others eased him into the bed, Rose climbed up with him, settling herself so his head could rest in her lap. Her fingers found his hair, her touch soothing even as his leg screamed.

At last, his brothers had Vincent draped over the back of his horse—apparently the way he'd made Rose ride out here, like cargo—and tied securely in place.

Thomas climbed onto the wagon bench and guided the team in a slow back-and-forth to turn the rig around in the cramped space. At last, they faced the trail back to Walnut Springs, and Robert climbed up into the wagon bed with James and Rose. He sat facing the three saddle horses tied to the back of the wagon, including the one bearing Vincent, and kept his rifle in his lap where it would be easy enough to lift and shoot should a threat arise.

The wagon lurched forward, and James bit hard on his lip to keep from crying out. He forced his breathing to stay even, forced his face to remain still despite the sweat dampening his collar. Rose had been through enough. Watching him fall apart wouldn't help her.

Her fingers wove through his hair in gentle strokes, and he focused on that instead of the pain. On the warmth of her lap beneath his head.

On the fact that she was alive, safe, and had agreed to marry him despite everything.

After what felt like hours, Rose lowered her head to speak quietly in his ear. "We're coming up on Walnut Springs."

He wanted to sit up, to see the town for himself, but his body refused to cooperate. The pain in his leg had settled into a constant throb that made even the smallest movement feel impossible. He settled for turning his head a little, just enough to catch a glimpse of the buildings above the wagon's side rails.

The familiar shapes of Walnut Springs emerged from the morning fog—the mercantile's weathered facade, the saloon's hanging sign, the boarding house where Vincent had found Rose.

His chest tightened again. How close he'd come to losing her again—maybe even forever.

Thomas guided the team down the main street, and a few townspeople braving the cold morning stopped to stare. Word would spread fast—the Balfour brothers returning at dawn with one of them laid out in the wagon bed and a man tied to a horse like a criminal.

Let them stare. Let them talk. Rose was safe, and that was all that mattered.

The wagon rolled to a stop in front of the jail, and Thomas spoke from the bench. "Robert, I'll tell the deputy what's going on if you want to see if the doc's in town."

Robert vaulted over the side of the wagon, his boots hitting the packed snow with a soft crunch. He strode toward the doctor's office, his long legs eating up the distance in seconds.

James tried to focus on something other than the fire in his leg—the way Rose's fingers still moved through his hair, the cold morning air against his face, the muffled voices of Thomas and the deputy as they discussed Vincent's crimes. But the pain kept pulling him under, waves of it that made his stomach churn and his vision blur.

Rose's hand stilled in his hair. "James?"

"Still here." The words scraped past his raw throat.

Her expression softened, but worry creased the corners of her eyes. He wanted to tell her he'd be fine, that this was nothing, but the lie wouldn't form.

Boot steps approached the wagon, and Dr. Morrison's lined face appeared above the side rail. His sharp eyes took in James's splinted leg, the torn trousers, the swelling that had turned the limb into something barely recognizable.

"Let's have a look." His tone was matter-of-fact, kind even, but the way his jaw tightened told James everything he needed to know about how bad it looked.

Still, before they did anything, he needed to know about… He pushed the words through the rocks in his throat. "Mandie? And the baby?"

Doc's expression softened, just a fraction, and some of the tension eased in James's chest. "Mother and baby are both well. A healthy little girl, born just after midnight. Enoch was near useless through the whole thing, but Mrs. Wang kept everyone fed and calm."

A girl. Mandie had delivered a girl, and both were safe. The relief that washed through him felt almost as powerful as the pain radiating from his leg.

"That's good." He almost managed a smile. "Real good."

Dr. Morrison nodded, then turned his attention back to James's leg. "Now let's see what you've done to yourself this time."

The next hour or so passed in a blur. His brothers and the doctor carrying him in, laying him in the exam room. Doc must have given him more laudanum, for his head turned to that foggy mud he had to fight to pull a thought through. At least the throbbing in his leg faded to a dull ache that was almost bearable compared to what it had been.

Voices drifted around him—Thomas's low murmur as he spoke with the deputy, Rose's soft replies to questions someone asked. He caught fragments of conversation, pieces that didn't quite fit together into a coherent whole.

"…broken in two places now…"

"…stay off it completely…"

"…weeks, maybe months…"

The words should have alarmed him, but the laudanum wrapped everything in cotton, softening the edges until even bad news felt distant and unimportant.

Another voice drifted in with the others. Was that…Bill? His surname wouldn't come. The man who'd stayed on their ranch, helping with the hay. The last time James had heard that voice… he'd been…drunk.

Now his tone sounded so very sober. Maybe even desperate.

James forced himself to focus on the words.

"…if I'd known, I would never…so sorry… said her family just wanted her back safe…" Bill's voice cracked. "I didn't know he was hurting her. Didn't know about her mama or—" He broke off. "I'm sorry, Miss Prescott. More sorry than I can say."

James blinked and shifted his head to see the cluster of figures. Rose stood with Thomas and Robert flanking her. The deputy. Bill.

The latter reached into his coat pocket and pulled out a wad —bills, folded and crumpled. "You take the money. What's left of it." He swallowed hard. "I didn't mean to hurt you. I promise."

Rose's expression shifted—that gentle steadiness he loved so much making her smile look almost serene. "I don't want the money, Mr. Carter. Keep it, or use it for something good." She slid a look toward James. Just a glance, but it fed his soul in ways he'd craved for years. "I have all I need here."

She turned back to Turner, whose hand had started to tremble.

His throat worked as he swallowed, then he nodded and stuffed the wad back into his coat. "I'll do that, ma'am. You have my word. And I'm so sorry again. If there's anything I can do. Ever. You just tell me."

"I appreciate that." Rose's voice carried the weight of everything she'd been through, but also something lighter—hope, maybe, or the beginning of healing.

James let his eyes drift closed again, the laudanum pulling him back toward the depths where the pain couldn't quite reach him. The voices continued around him, distant now, like he was underwater and they were speaking from the surface.

Then a hand closed around his—small, familiar. Rose's soft, cool fingers threaded through his, and even through the haze of medicine, the touch anchored him.

He let himself relax, let himself rest in her hold and the peace that only God could bring. The last thing he felt was the sweet brush of Rose's kiss on his forehead.

# CHAPTER 33

At Rose's first glimpse of the ranch house through the pines, so many emotions flooded her, tightening her throat so she couldn't have spoken if she tried. Those familiar log walls and steep-pitched roof rising against the mountain backdrop looked more like home than any place she'd ever known.

Two days ago—was it really only two days?—she'd run from this place, convinced James would blame her for Vincent's poison seeping into his family. Convinced she didn't deserve the life spreading before her. A gift she had no right to accept.

Now, beside her in the wagon bed, James squeezed her hand. She met his gaze, letting herself sink into that smile—tired as it was—and the love shimmering past the hint of pain that still lingered in his eyes.

They'd stayed one night in Walnut Springs, giving his body a rest before this final leg of the journey home.

*This* was home. These people her family.

The wagon rolled into the yard, and movement on the porch pulled her attention. Bea stepped out first, her small frame wrapped in a thick shawl against the cold. Then Mandie appeared behind her, and Rose's chest expanded with so much relief.

Mandie looked wonderful—pale perhaps, a little unsteady on her feet as she gripped the door.

But whole. Alive. The round swell of pregnancy had diminished, replaced by the soft curves of a woman who'd just brought new life into the world.

Where *was* the babe?

Thomas reined the team to a stop, and Rose was already moving, climbing over the side of the wagon before anyone could help her down. When her boots hit the packed snow, she stumbled—her legs stiff from the cold ride—but caught herself.

And then Bea was there, pulling her into a fierce hug that smelled of bread and wood smoke and safety.

"Foolish girl." The words came out rough against Rose's hair. "Running off like that. Had us all worried sick."

Her eyes burned as she let herself sink into the embrace, breathing in that familiar scent of comfort and belonging. "I'm sorry. I'm so sorry."

"Shh." Bea pulled back just enough to cup Rose's face in her weathered hands, her dark eyes scanning every bruise, every mark Vincent had left behind. Her expression shifted—softened and hardened all at once—and her thumb brushed across Rose's cheekbone. "You're home now. That's what matters."

That word again. Home. How could four little letters mean so much?

"My turn." Mandie touched her shoulder.

Bea pulled back with a chuckle as Mandie closed in.

Her arms came around Rose in a careful hug, gentler than Bea's fierce embrace, but no less meaningful.

"Thank God you're safe." Mandie's whisper warmed Rose's ear. "Now that I finally have a sister, I couldn't stand the thought of losing you."

*Sister.* Rose had to blink hard against fresh tears. She'd never had family beyond her mother, and even that had been stolen away too soon. Now so many people she would soon call family.

Behind them drifted the sounds of Thomas and Robert helping James down from the wagon. His sharp intake of breath cut through her overwhelming emotions. He needed to be inside, resting that twice-broken leg.

She pulled back and sniffed to rein in her composure. "Where's the babe? And Enoch?"

Mandie turned to the front door, which stood ajar. "Come in and see them. It's so cold out here, Enoch didn't want her in the wind."

Rose almost chuckled. She could certainly imagine Enoch would be protective of his new daughter.

James was already hobbling up the porch steps, a brother helping on either side. She waited to enter with him. She wasn't even real kin to Mandie's baby, so she shouldn't be the first to see her.

But James motioned for her to step in before them, the corners of his eyes creasing in a smile that said he knew how much she wanted to hurry inside.

The warmth of the great room wrapped around her. The familiar scents—pine logs and wood smoke and something baking in the kitchen—settled into her lungs, and another wave of emotion threatened to undo her completely.

Mandie crossed to her husband, and the sight of him nearly stopped Rose's breathing.

The big rancher—Lord Enoch Balfour, heir apparent to the Duke of Clarence—cradled a tiny bundle against his broad chest, his large hands supporting the infant with such reverence, such tenderness. Something warm and bright unfurled through her chest.

He looked down at the baby with an expression she'd never seen on his usually guarded face—a wonder so raw it trembled in the lines around his mouth, tangled with the fierce protectiveness that was Enoch to the core.

This wasn't his child by blood. James had told her that much during one of their conversations at the ranch, explained in careful words about the awful thing that had been done to Mandie before she'd ever found her way here, before she ever met Enoch.

But the love shining in his eyes now could only belong to a father gazing at his newborn daughter.

Maybe blood didn't matter as much as everyone always said it did. Maybe family was built out of love, sacrifice, and being there when it mattered most. Not simply born—it was chosen.

Behind her, James's walking sticks tapped against the floor as his brothers helped him inside. He came to a stop beside her, and she glanced up at him. His eyes glistened as he took in his brother.

What a perfect family they made. Enoch and Mandie and the babe that was theirs to treasure.

James nudged Rose forward, and Enoch shifted a little, angling the babe so she could see.

The infant's face was perfect—round and pink, with a dusting of dark hair peeking from beneath a knitted cap. Her eyes were closed, her tiny mouth working in sleep, and one miniature fist had escaped the blankets to curl against Enoch's chest.

That tiny fist, so impossibly small it could barely wrap around one of Enoch's fingers. How could anyone look at such perfect innocence and not want to protect it with everything inside them?

"Would you like to hold her?" Mandie's voice came out warm with an invitation that made Rose's throat close up again.

She wanted to say yes. Wanted it so badly her arms ached with the emptiness. But her hands were still trembling from the cold ride. And... "I...I've never..."

Mandie's smile deepened, and she reached out to squeeze Rose's arm. "She's practically begging for her auntie to hold her."

Enoch moved closer, and Rose found herself accepting the precious weight as he transferred his daughter into her arms. The baby settled against her chest, warm and solid despite her tiny size, and Rose's throat tightened until she could barely breathe.

She'd never held an infant before. Never had the chance, locked up so tight in Vincent's grip.

The baby shifted a little, her tiny face scrunching up before relaxing back into sleep.

Something inside Rose shifted too—cracked open and spilled over with an emotion so powerful it freed her tears once more.

She moved carefully toward the settee where James was settling himself, his brothers helping ease him down. They lifted his splinted leg to rest on the table before him.

She had to share this moment with him, needed him to see what she was feeling, even if she couldn't find words for it.

Once he was situated, she lowered herself beside him, angling the babe so they could both see her tiny features. The firelight caught the downy dark hair, made her skin glow golden and perfect.

"We named her Catherine." Mandie said from where she stood with Enoch. "After your mother, James, Lady Balfour."

The name pierced straight through Rose's already fragile composure. Catherine. Lady Catherine Balfour, the woman who'd shown such kindness to a common nine-year-old girl all those years ago. The woman whose gentle grace had left its mark on all her sons, teaching them what love looked like even when the world grew hard.

The tears flowed hot down her cheeks as she gazed at the tiny face nestled in her arms. This precious child would carry forward that legacy of kindness and strength, would grow up knowing she was loved and wanted and cherished.

James's hand found hers where it supported Catherine's small body, his fingers threading through hers. Anchoring her.

She looked up at him. He was watching the baby with such tenderness, such wonder—his battered features softened, the pain lines around his mouth easing as he studied his tiny niece.

Then his gaze lifted to meet hers, and the love shining there reached so deep inside her chest she could barely contain it. Whether she deserved it or not…this love was real.

And it was hers.

God had given her all these gifts—given her James, this family, this future she'd never dared to imagine during all those dark years.

"Would you like to hold her?" She kept her voice soft so she didn't wake the sleeping infant. But James needed to experience this weight in his arms. This promise of what their own future might hold.

His smile reached all the way to his eyes despite the exhaustion pulling at his features. "I'd love to."

She helped transfer the tiny bundle into his arms, careful not to jostle his injured leg. He settled Catherine against his chest with a natural ease that surprised her—this man who'd spent his life working cattle and breaking horses somehow knew exactly how to cradle an infant like she was made of spun glass.

The sight of him—her strong husband-to-be, her best friend in all the world—holding his tiny niece with such gentleness stirred something deep and warm through her chest. Something that felt almost too big to contain.

One day, Lord willing, they would have their own babe. Maybe several of them, filling this house with laughter and noise and the beautiful chaos of family. She'd never let herself imagine such a thing before.

But God was proving His love wasn't conditional. Wasn't

dependent on what had happened to her or how she'd responded. He simply loved her—the way James loved her—completely and without conditions.

Rose leaned into him, resting her head against his shoulder as they both gazed at little Catherine. The warmth of the fire reached her now, seeping into her bones after the cold journey.

The familiar sounds of the ranch house settled around them —Thomas speaking with Enoch in low tones, Bea's footsteps moving toward the kitchen, Mandie's soft laugh at something Robert said.

The sounds of family. Of home.

This future—this life—she would treasure every single day for as long as God gave her breath.

# EPILOGUE

The winter sunlight streaming through the great room windows caught the delicate lace of Rose's dress. His mother's dress. The sight of it stung James's eyes more than he'd expected, a sudden burn that made him blink, hard, before he could quite steady himself.

A week. Only a single week since his leg had been broken in two places instead of one, Vincent had been locked away, and they'd returned to the ranch. Doc Morrison had urged him to wait longer before their wedding. To rest. To let his body mend before daring to stand so long.

But no. He couldn't. He wouldn't.

He would stand for his bride. Would speak his vows on his own two feet—broken leg and all—because Rose deserved all of him. His full attention, his steadiness, his stubborn, unrelenting devotion. If it took every bit of strength he had, so be it.

The walking sticks bit into his armpits as he shifted his weight, trying to ease the pressure on his splinted leg. The pain was there—a constant throb—but it felt distant somehow, unimportant compared to the woman moving toward him through the great room.

Rose.

His Rose, finally.

Mrs. Wang had worked a kind of magic with the alterations, taking his mother's wedding dress and somehow fitting it to Rose's smaller shape so perfectly it looked as if the dress had always belonged to her. The cream silk shifted and shimmered with every step Rose took. The scent of pine boughs and red berries, gathered from the same forests where he and Rose had played as children, filled the air with the scent of the mountains they both loved.

Her auburn hair had been arranged in soft waves that framed her face, and someone—Mandie, probably—had woven tiny white flowers through the strands. But it was Rose's eyes that held him captive. Those green eyes that had haunted his dreams for eleven long years looked at him with a love so fierce it took his breath away.

No wariness. No fear. Just that fierce, clear love—real and nearly blinding in its strength.

She reached him, and his brother Enoch—who stood beside him as his best man—stepped back to give them space. The room fell silent except for the crackle of the fire and baby Catherine's soft breathing from her cradle near Mandie's chair.

James let himself sink into Rose's gaze as Sheriff Hawkins began the ceremony. The words washed over him—familiar phrases about love and commitment, about choosing each other through joy and sorrow, through sickness and health. Each phrase circled them, settling in the hush, until all else faded except the promise passing between them.

When it came time for his vows, he had to clear his throat twice before the words would come. He'd warned Rose he planned to add a little to the end of the vows. A few promises especially for her.

He started with the old words, steady as the sheriff spoke them, repeating everything in turn. Then he pressed his thumb along the back of her hand and fixed his gaze on her. "Rose, I vow to love you for the rest of my life. To protect you with everything I have. To stand beside you through whatever storms may come."

The words he'd practiced tumbled out. "I vow to never let a day pass without reminding you how precious you are, how deeply you're loved. And I promise that no matter what the future holds, you will always—always—have a home with me."

Tears spilled down her cheeks, but her smile never wavered. She repeated her own vows as the sheriff spoke them, then her sweet voice broke from the pattern, softer and even more certain.

"James Balfour, I vow to stay. To build a life here with you, to never run away again, no matter how frightening the truth might be." Her fingers curled tighter around his, holding on. "I vow to trust you, to trust God, and to trust that the love we share is strong enough to weather anything. You've been my best friend, my protector, my home. Now you'll be my husband, and I promise to cherish that gift every day for the rest of my life."

So much love, so much joy surged inside him, his own tears wouldn't stay back.

The sheriff's final words—"You may kiss your bride"—barely registered before James was leaning forward, his walking sticks threatening to slip as he claimed Rose's mouth with his own.

She tasted of contentment and sweetness and a future he hardly dared picture, and when she kissed him back, so gentle it hollowed out his chest, the pain in his leg faded to something distant, unimportant.

He could almost forget his brothers were surely grinning behind him, taking in every second. All that mattered was this one moment, the promise of her mouth against his, the way joy and ache collided so sharply he was left only wanting more.

The celebration that followed blurred together—Mrs. Wang's feast spread across the dining table, Thomas's toast that made everyone laugh and Rose blush, Robert's more serious words about new beginnings and God's faithfulness. And finally, Enoch's quiet congratulations, softer than the rest, but somehow ringing truer, larger, echoing for him above all the rest.

But it was the quiet moments James treasured most. Watching Rose cradle Catherine while Mandie ate, the way his wife's—his *wife's*—face softened as she gazed at the sleeping infant. The wonder in her eyes when Catherine's tiny fist wrapped around her aunt's finger.

He couldn't change the past. Couldn't erase the years Vincent had stolen from them or undo the scars that monster had left on Rose's heart. But he could give her this—a future filled with love and family and the promise of their own children someday.

He would spend every day forward making sure Rose knew just how loved and cherished she was.

As the afternoon wore on, the conversation around the table turned to the letter that had arrived from their father three days ago. Robert pulled it from his coat pocket and unfolded it, reading aloud the portion about their coming royal guest.

"A cousin of the queen is planning a hunting expedition to the American West next month. Father requests that at least one of us journey to Fort Benton to pay our respects on behalf of the family."

An awkward silence settled over the table. Fort Benton was a week's journey north, and with James's broken leg and Enoch preparing to leave for England in the summer, the timing couldn't be worse.

Thomas set down his coffee cup. "I'll go."

All eyes turned to him.

"You sure?" Enoch's voice carried a note of concern. "There will be a lot of pomp. A lot of frivolity and the endless need to compliment a man who likely couldn't hit a buffalo grazing on the plain."

Thomas shrugged, but something in his eyes suggested the decision went deeper than simple duty. "I could use some time away from the ranch anyway. See a bit more of the territory. Someone needs to represent the family, and you all have more pressing matters here." He nodded toward James's splinted leg and Enoch's wife and newborn daughter.

James studied his youngest brother. A kind of restless energy that had been building in Thomas for months now. Maybe the journey would do him good. Give him space to sort through whatever was weighing on his mind.

"All right then." Enoch nodded. "We'll make the arrangements."

The conversation shifted to lighter topics after that, but Thomas didn't join in. He stared out the window, his thoughts far away. Whatever his brother was running from—or running toward—James could only pray he'd find what he needed in Fort Benton.

Later, as the afternoon light began to fade and baby Catherine woke demanding to be fed again, James hobbled into the kitchen for a few minutes alone with Enoch. His eldest brother had come to make another pot of coffee, and James now sank into a chair at the table. He needed a moment away from the celebration to rest his screaming leg and perhaps steal a few quiet words with his brother.

Times like this, he missed Will so deep, it felt like the pain would never fade. How many times had he and Enoch and Will stood here in this very room? Enoch sharp-tongued as ever, Will grinning, both of them doubling up to tease him over some fool thing he'd said or done.

He'd pretended to resent their jabs back then, but now he'd give anything to hear Will's laugh again. He'd always looked up to his brothers, always would. And this ache felt like it might never fade.

Enoch lifted the lid on the pot to check the brewing coffee inside. "I think it's ready."

"Smells good. Mrs. Wang outdid herself with everything today."

Enoch nodded, pouring two fresh cups of the brew. "She's been planning this feast all week." He handed one to James, then settled in the chair nearest him, his expression thoughtful. "I'm happy for you, brother. Rose is good for you. Always has been."

"Thank you." The words burrowed deep, warming far more than the coffee ever could.

Enoch took a sip, then set his cup down carefully. "The sheriff brought our mail when he came for the ceremony." He pulled a folded letter from his pocket. "This came from Judge Harrison."

James's pulse quickened as he took the paper. Robert had traveled to Helena earlier this week for a preliminary discussion with the judge in Helena who'd been one of Father's contacts. The man had promised to review the details and advise them how he'd like to proceed.

James scanned the script, but then forced himself to slow and read every word:

Lord Balfour,

I have reviewed the contract and supporting documents you brought to me. From what I can determine, this agreement is unconscionable and unenforceable under territorial law. A contract signed by a minor under duress, particularly one demanding twenty years of servitude, violates fundamental principles of justice.

With regards to Mr. Dunhill's recent activities, the evidence for kidnapping is irrefutable, and the charges of extortion and fraud related to Miss Prescott's contract should also stand. The matter of Lady Balfour's death remains more difficult to prove, given the passage of time and lack of physical evidence, but even without that charge, Mr. Dunhill will spend many years in prison.

I look forward to seeing justice served in this matter.

Respectfully,
Judge Marcus Harrison

Relief flooded through James so powerfully his hands trembled. He looked up at his brother, who was watching him carefully.

"Rose doesn't know yet." Enoch spoke quietly. "We thought you should be the one to tell her."

James nodded, refolding the letter and tucking it into his pocket. "Thanks." He'd find the right time. Then they would savor the knowledge that Vincent's hold on Rose was truly, legally broken.

He eyed his brother. "Are you looking forward to going to England next summer? After Mandie and Catherine are stronger?" None of them had ever been back, not since they first came here. Enoch had been six at the time. James four, almost five. No matter how hard he'd tried through the years, he couldn't remember anything from what most people called their homeland.

These mountains felt like home. All his memories lived here. His future too, Lord willing.

Something flicked across Enoch's face—not quite reluctance, but close. He stared into his mug, then sighed. "I'm resigned to it. It's my responsibility, as the eldest now." He looked up, meeting James's gaze. "But it's still going to be hard to leave these mountains. This is home in a way England never will be."

James understood that feeling in his bones. These mountains, this ranch—they'd shaped all of them into who they were. Leaving, even temporarily, would be like cutting away a piece of themselves.

And they all knew that Enoch's move likely wouldn't be temporary. The responsibilities of the Duke of Clarence required daily work, especially when Parliament was in session.

They sat in silence for a moment, thick with a host of memories and plans.

Then Enoch pushed to his feet and set his empty cup on the counter. "Come on. Your bride is probably wondering where you've disappeared to."

He was right. When they returned to the great room, Rose's eyes immediately found James's, and the smile that lit her face made his chest tighten all over again.

The celebration continued into the evening, but eventually his family all drifted to their own rooms.

Mrs. Wang was the last to go, pressing a kiss to Rose's cheek and whispering something in her ear that made Rose's eyes shine with fresh tears. Then Mrs. Wang disappeared into her own quarters, leaving them alone at last.

The house settled into quiet around them—just the crackle of the dying fire and the soft sounds of the ranch at rest. Rose moved to stand beside him where he leaned against the mantel, and he pulled her close against his side. She wrapped her arms around his waist, snuggling in.

"It was a beautiful day," she said softly.

"The most beautiful."

She clung a little tighter. "Do you know what amazes me most?"

"What?" Emotion clogged his throat.

"How God can take something so broken—like my years with Vincent, like your broken leg—and use it to create something beautiful. He's redeeming the years Vincent stole and giving us a future I never dreamed possible."

This woman. How could she be so wise, so strong, and yet still so gentle?

He pressed a kiss into her hair, breathing in the sweet scent of her. "I think sometimes God's best gifts come wrapped in our deepest pain. My broken leg forced me to hand over control to God. Your time with Vincent, horrible as it was, taught you strength I never could have given you. And now—" He smiled. "Now we get to spend the rest of our lives discovering what God does with people who've learned to trust Him."

"The rest of our lives." Contentment laced her voice as her shoulders rose and fell in a long breath.

Then she pulled back enough to look up at him.

He took the opportunity to brush his mouth over hers. Not the light touch of public vows, not a gesture for others to witness, but something deeper—a quiet exchange, just for them. A promise, unvoiced but certain, that their new life started now. Here, in this moment.

When they finally pulled apart, Rose's cheeks were flushed and her breathing unsteady. "We should probably..." She glanced toward the stairs, toward his room that now belonged to them both.

"Probably." But he didn't move yet. Just stood there holding her, memorizing this moment. The way the firelight caught in her hair. The love shining in her eyes. The peace settling over them both.

He couldn't stop every storm or heal his own broken bone. But he could lay the ones he loved into God's hands and keep his arms open. Maybe that was what strength truly was—not the ability to control or fix everything, but the wisdom to trust the Father instead of trying to handle it all alone.

"Ready?" Rose's soft question pulled him back to the present.

He grinned. "I've been ready for eleven years."

She laughed—that beautiful sound he'd been afraid he'd never hear again—and helped him navigate the stairs to their room.

* * *

I pray you loved James and Rose's story!

Would you like to receive a **free bonus epilogue of their a peek at their happily ever after AND a glimpse at the trouble Thomas gets into during the hunting expedition with the queen's cousin**?
Get the bonus epilogue and sign-up for insider email updates at https://mistymbeller.com/MOB-bonus-epilogue

* * *

Then make sure you grab book 3 in the series for Thomas's full story. As you can image, it's quite a doozy!

* Mail-order bride gone wrong
* Snowed-in/forced proximity
* Marriage of convenience

Turn the page for a sneak peek of *Mail-Order Viscountess,* book 3 in the Lords of the Rockies series!

# SNEAK PEEK: MAIL-ORDER VISCOUNTESS

**Chapter One**

FEBRUARY, 1870
BUTTE, MONTANA TERRITORY

The crate hit the wagon bed with a satisfying thud, and Thomas Balfour scraped a sleeve across his forehead as he turned for another. The morning sun had climbed higher over Butte's ice-hardened streets, melting some areas into slush. Though his breath still formed small clouds as he moved, loading supplies for the ranch had burned through the cold in his limbs.

The physical exertion felt good. Better than standing still. Better than thinking.

"That's it for the baking goods." His brother James hefted another wooden box alongside where Thomas placed his. "Mrs. Wang will be happy about these spices they didn't have last time."

Thomas grunted and pushed a crate of nails and tools in next to the others.

James had been acting strange all morning—cheerful in that

forced way that meant he was hiding something. And James's wife, Rose, had been glancing at Thomas with an expression he couldn't quite read. Pity, maybe. Or concern.

Were they hiding something from him?

The mercantile's back door stood propped open despite the cold, and Rose's voice sounded from inside, discussing fabric with the shopkeeper.

It didn't seem like all three of them had needed to come on this supply run, especially since Butte lay a full day's wagon ride from their ranch.

Thomas could have handled it alone, or James and Rose could have made a holiday of it—newlyweds that they were.

But his brother had insisted. Something about having help if the weather turned bad and the road became impassable. At least coming to town had given Thomas the chance to order the last supplies he'd need for the trip west.

He gripped the edge of another crate and hauled it toward him. The wood bit into his palms even through his work gloves.

"Thomas." James's voice came from too close behind him. "Leave that one. We need to talk."

The hair on the back of his neck prickled. What now?

"Plenty of time for talking on the ride home." He grabbed the box and swung it up. "Still got half a wagon to fill."

"The supplies can wait."

Something in James's tone made Thomas drop the crate into the bed harder than necessary. He turned and pulled off his gloves. "What about?"

James shifted his weight, glanced back toward the mercantile door, then met Thomas's eyes. "There's a reason we wanted you to come with us to Butte."

"Obviously." Thomas crossed his arms. Now they'd finally get down to it.

James scrubbed a hand through his hair—the movement he always did when preparing to deliver bad news.

"Just say it." Thomas leaned against the wagon, crossing one boot over the other in a show of casualness to hide the clenching in his gut.

"We've, um… We thought… That is, Enoch, Robert, and I discussed it, and we felt…"

"Spit it out, James."

His brother's shoulders straightened, taking on that older-brother-knows-best posture Thomas had learned to despise. "You've been different since the knighting ceremony. Restless. Taking more risks than usual." James held up a hand before Thomas could protest. "Don't deny it. That business with that three-year-old stallion last month? You could have been killed."

"But I wasn't." He kept his voice level, though it took everything inside him. "I broke the horse, and now he's bringing a good price from that rancher in Helena."

"That's not the point."

"Then what is the point, James?" He spat the words. "You brought me all the way to Butte to lecture me about my horse training methods?"

Rose stepped from the mercantile, a wrapped parcel in her arms. Her face blanched when she saw them, and the look she and James exchanged stoked the fire burning in his chest.

This had nothing to do with horse training.

James turned back to him, and his voice dropped to a no-nonsense tone. "We've arranged something. Something we think will be good for you."

*Arranged something.*

Thomas could count on one hand the number of times his brothers had arranged anything for him that turned out well. Usually their planning involved more responsibility at the ranch, more reasons to stay put, more ways to keep him from the life he actually wanted. A life in California.

"What kind of something?" He clenched his jaw to keep his anger in check.

"A bride."

The world tilted sideways for a moment. He had to have heard wrong. "A what?"

"A mail-order bride. She's arriving on the afternoon stage."

The words burned in the cold air between them.

Thomas stared at his brother. He had to have misheard.

The sounds of Butte filtered through—a wagon rattling past on the street, someone shouting about fresh deer meat, hammer on metal at the smithy.

Normal sounds. Ordinary sounds.

But James had said something impossible.

Thomas finally forced out words. "A what?"

"A mail-order bride. For you."

A mail-order bride. What in the Bitterroot Mountains were they thinking?

His brothers had summoned a woman all the way out here, presumably from back East, and hadn't bothered to ask him first?

Heat flooded through him, flaring hot and fast. The nerve of them. The absolute gall.

"No." The word came out flat. Final.

James stepped closer, hands raised in that placating gesture that made Thomas want to hit something. "Just listen. We're worried about you. Ever since you came back from Fort Benton with that new title, you've been—"

"Been what? Myself?" Thomas pushed off from the wagon. "Sorry if that's inconvenient for you all."

"You've been reckless. Talking about California, about leaving. Taking risks that could get you killed."

"So you bought me a wife?" The absurdity of it choked him. "You think shackling me to some stranger is going to make me want to stay?"

"Marriage settles a man." James glanced at his wife. "Gives him something to live for. Something to—"

"I don't need settling." Thomas clenched his hands into fists. "I need to be left alone to live my own life."

"You don't know what you need." Rose spoke for the first time, her voice gentle but firm. She set down her parcel in the wagon bed. "Thomas, I understand how you feel. Truly, I do. But sometimes the very thing we think will trap us is actually the thing that sets us free."

He barked out a laugh. "That's easy to say when you chose your husband. When you had a say in your own future."

The hit landed—he saw it in the way Rose's face tightened—and a sliver of remorse slid through him. Given her past, that was an especially low blow.

Yet his chest felt like it might crack open. His brothers had betrayed him. All of them. Enoch, Robert, *and* James. Even their wives, and probably Mrs. Wang too.

They'd sat around discussing his life, his *future*, as if he were a problem to be solved rather than a man with his own mind. Sure, he was the youngest in the family, but how incapable did they think him?

"When does this stage arrive?" The words tasted bitter.

James glanced at the sun's position. "Three hours. Maybe four."

Three hours until some unsuspecting woman showed up looking for her new husband. A husband who hadn't asked for her, didn't want her, and sure as Montana winters were cold wouldn't marry her.

"You'll send her back." He grabbed his gloves from where he'd dropped them and started toward the main street.

"We can't do that." James moved to block his path. "She's traveled all this way. Given up everything—"

"Not my problem." Thomas shouldered past him. "I didn't invite her. I didn't write to her. I didn't make any promises to her. You did."

The rage felt good—clean and hot and righteous. Better than

the hollow feeling that had been eating at him for months. Ever since that ill-fated event in Fort Benton with the queen's cousin that ended up in him being knighted—for failing to protect a man.

He stomped down the alley between buildings, splashing through half-frozen puddles. The main street of Butte stretched before him, crowded with freight wagons and miners and the usual chaos of a mining town flush with silver money.

Somewhere in this mess of humanity, there had to be a saloon. Not that he'd drink more than coffee. He'd never been able to stand that rot-gut whiskey. But he needed to lose himself somewhere.

James called after him, but Thomas didn't turn back.

James, of all people, should have understood. James had been the one who listened when Thomas talked about California, about starting fresh somewhere nobody knew the Balfour name or cared about English titles that meant nothing out here. James had nodded and said he understood the restlessness.

Apparently understanding and respecting were two different things.

Thomas shouldered past a group of miners arguing about claim boundaries. The smell of unwashed bodies and stale tobacco smoke hung thick in the winter air.

A painted sign swung from chains ahead—The Silver Strike. Good enough.

The interior was dim after the bright winter sunlight, and Thomas paused inside the door to let his eyes adjust. The place reeked of whiskey and sawdust, with an undertone of something sharper. Cigar smoke, maybe, or the particular desperation that clung to men who spent their days underground working for barely enough to survive on.

A handful of men clustered around tables, nursing drinks despite the early hour. A few glanced up at his entrance, their gazes watching—the way men in rough towns always sized up strangers.

He ignored them and headed for the bar.

The barkeep, a grizzled man with more scars than teeth, wiped at a glass with a rag that looked dirtier than the glass itself. "What'll it be?"

"Coffee. If you have it." He'd need his wits to get out of this mess. Especially without saying or doing something he'd regret to James.

One eyebrow climbed toward the man's receding hairline. "Coffee."

"That a problem?"

"No problem at all." The man set down the glass and turned toward a pot sitting on a small stove behind the counter. "Just don't get many asking for it."

Thomas leaned against the bar and tried to let the anger drain out of him.

It wasn't working.

Every time he thought about James's face—that earnest, we-know-what's-best-for-you expression—the fury climbed higher in his throat.

A mail-order bride. As if he were some pathetic bachelor too inept to find his own wife. As if he even wanted a wife.

The bartender slid a chipped mug across the scarred wood. The coffee inside looked thick enough to stand a spoon in and smelled like it had been sitting on that stove since yesterday. Perfect.

Thomas wrapped his hands around the mug's warmth and stared into the dark liquid. Somewhere a few miles from here, a woman traveled toward a future that didn't exist. Some poor soul who'd believed the letters his brothers had written—probably full of descriptions of the ranch, the mountains, the life she could have here.

All lies.

Well, not lies exactly. The ranch existed. The mountains were real enough.

But the husband? That was pure fiction.

He took a sip of the coffee. It tasted as bad as it looked—bitter and burnt—but at least it gave him something to do with his hands besides put them through a wall.

"Trouble with a woman?"

Thomas glanced sideways. The bartender had returned to his glass-wiping, though his attention remained fixed on Thomas with the knowing look of a man who'd seen every kind of misery parade through his establishment.

"Something like that."

"Always is." The man chuckled, a sound like gravel in a tin can. "They're either the cause of your problems or the solution. Sometimes both."

Thomas didn't respond. The last thing he needed was philosophy from a saloon keeper.

What kind of woman agreed to marry a stranger sight unseen anyway? Someone desperate, probably. Or running from something.

That thought pricked his conscience. She came all this way, expecting...what? A home? Security? Love, even?

He shoved the thought aside. Not his problem. He hadn't made her any promises.

He had his own plans.

California. Only a few more weeks before he'd have his supplies gathered and be ready to head out. Stake a claim on his own land. Start his own ranch.

His own future. Not one mapped out by his brothers or dictated by family duty or trapped by some English title he'd never asked for.

A burst of laughter erupted from a corner table, harsh and mean-edged.

He glanced over. Four men sat hunched around a table in the

corner, cards spread between them. The kind of men who looked like they'd been in Butte too long—faces hard with disappointment, clothes worn past decent.

One of them had a woman on his lap. She couldn't have been more than eighteen, dressed in a faded calico dress that had seen better days. Her eyes darted around the room like a trapped animal looking for escape, and her smile was fixed in place with the brittle quality of something about to shatter.

The man holding her had one meaty hand clamped around her wrist, his other arm wrapped tight across her waist. He said something Thomas couldn't make out, and his companions roared with laughter. The girl's smile never wavered, but her fingers clutched at the edge of the table until her knuckles went white.

He should look away. Not his business. Butte was full of hard men and women trying to survive however they could. He couldn't solve everyone else's problems when he couldn't even settle his own.

The girl's face had gone pale beneath the rouge on her cheeks.

Thomas set down his coffee mug.

"Those aren't men you want to cross." The bartender's voice held an unmistakable warning.

"I'm just going to have a friendly word." He was already moving away from the bar. The anger burning in his chest since James's revelation found a new target, and he welcomed the shift.

He could actually do something about this situation.

The four men didn't look up as he approached their table. Too focused on their cards and their captive audience.

Up close, the girl looked even younger—maybe sixteen. A smudge of dirt marked her jaw beneath the powder, and the dress hung loose on her thin frame. Her eyes flicked to Thomas for a half second, and something in that look—hope mixed with terror—made his jaw tighten.

"Gentlemen." He kept his voice easy, his posture relaxed. He'd learned years ago that the appearance of calm could diffuse most any situation. "Wondering if I might borrow the lady for a moment."

The man holding the girl finally looked up. His face wore hard angles and old scars, with eyes that had gone flat from too much whiskey or too much disappointment. Probably both. "We're in the middle of a game."

"I can see that." Thomas smiled—the charming, harmless smile that made people underestimate him. "Won't take but a minute. The lady's employer is looking for her."

"Her employer?" The man tugged the girl a little, and she winced. "That would be Nelson, and he's right here."

Thomas slid his gaze to the man he'd called Nelson—a wiry fellow with thinning hair and a mouth like a knife slash. The one who'd laughed loudest at whatever crude joke had been made.

Nelson eyed him, a gleam in his eyes that said he might be willing to hand her off to Thomas if that increased the profit in his pocket for the girl's time. Would buying an hour—or an afternoon—really do much to help her though? She needed a new home. A new life. And he couldn't give her either. Probably.

Or could he? If he bought her freedom, would she have a place to go? Friends or family back East?

What was he thinking? He couldn't rescue every girl in every mining town saloon in the Montana Territory?

But the way her fingers trembled against the table edge...

"How much?" He pulled two coins from his pocket—money he'd brought to buy supplies for California, for a fresh start that apparently his brothers were determined to prevent.

Nelson's eyes lit up. "Depends on what you're wanting."

"Just her time. For the afternoon." The words tasted sour, but he kept his expression neutral. "I'll pay double your usual rate if you let her go now."

The man holding the girl—the one with the scarred face—tightened his grip. "We ain't done with her yet."

"Jake." Nelson leaned forward, his gaze fixed on the silver in Thomas's hand. "Let the man have what he's paying for."

"I said we ain't done."

The temperature in the room shifted—that moment when a situation teetered between resolution and violence. The other two men at the table had gone still, watching. Waiting to see which direction this would tip.

He'd talked his way out of worse situations than this. He could do it again.

"I'm not looking for trouble." He kept his hands visible, the money in his open palm. "Only want to spend some time with the lady. You'll get your cut, I'll get hers, and everyone walks away happy."

Jake's chair scraped against the floorboards as he stood, still gripping the girl. He was a big man—taller than Thomas by a few inches and built like someone who'd spent years swinging a pickaxe. The kind of size that usually ended arguments before they started.

Thomas didn't move. Just kept an easy smile in place.

The bar lay behind him—maybe eight strides away. The door to his left, blocked by another table. The other two men were still seated, but they'd be on their feet in seconds if this went bad.

"You think you can walk in here and take what you want?" Jake's breath hit his face, reeking of whiskey and decay.

"I think I offered fair payment for the lady's time." He shifted his weight a little, ready to move if needed. The girl had gone rigid in Jake's grip, her eyes wide. "I imagine Nelson will give your money back."

Jake's mouth twisted into something that might have been a smile on a friendlier face. "Maybe I don't want the money."

The other two men stood now. Chairs scraped across floorboards, the sound seemed far too loud in the sudden quiet. All other patrons had gone still, watching. Waiting.

His own pulse surged through his body, but he kept his breathing steady.

He'd been in worse spots than this. That time in Fort Benton when he'd accidentally insulted a trapper's wife. The cattle thieves two years ago. The stallion that had nearly crushed his ribs.

Though looking at Jake's fists—each roughly the size of a small ham—maybe this ranked higher on the list of stupid decisions than he'd initially thought.

"Then what do you want?" He kept his tone conversational, as if they were discussing the weather instead of standing on the edge of a brawl.

Jake released the girl with a shove that sent her stumbling against the table. She caught herself but didn't run.

Just stood there frozen, like a deer that had spotted the wolf but couldn't remember how to move.

"I want you to mind your own business." Jake stepped closer, crowding into Thomas's space. "And get out of my saloon."

*Was* it this man's saloon? Or did he simply spew big talk?

Still, retreating now would be like showing your back to a mean dog—it only made them bite harder.

Some distant part of his mind whispered that this might be exactly the kind of recklessness James had been talking about—walking into a situation that could get him killed over a girl he didn't know.

But he'd already opened his mouth. Already made the play. No backing down now.

"Actually..." He let his smile sharpen just enough to show

teeth. "I think this is exactly my business now. Seeing as I've already paid for the lady's time."

The first punch came faster than Thomas expected—a wild haymaker aimed at his jaw. He ducked sideways as the wind of it passed over his head. His shoulder crashed into the table edge, scattering cards and coins across the floor.

The girl screamed.

Thomas straightened in time to catch Jake's second swing on his forearm, the impact jarring all the way to his shoulder. Pain bloomed hot and immediate, but he shoved it aside and drove his fist into Jake's gut.

Like punching a barrel. The man barely grunted.

Then Jake's companions were moving. One grabbed Thomas's left arm, yanking it behind his back. The other came at him from the front, fist raised.

Thomas drove his boot down on the instep of the man holding him. Bones crunched, and the grip loosened enough for him to wrench free. He spun, using the momentum to throw an elbow that connected with someone's face. Cartilage gave way with a wet crunch.

Someone howled.

The room tilted as something slammed into the side of his head—Jake's fist, probably, though everything had gone a bit fuzzy around the edges.

Then the distant crack of a rifle echoed through the air.

Get MAIL-ORDER VISCOUNTESS, book 3 in the Lords of the Rockies series, at your favorite retailer!

Did you enjoy James and Rose's story? I hope so!
**Would you take a quick minute to leave a review where you purchased the book?**
It doesn't have to be long. Just a sentence or two telling what you liked about the story!

* * *

To receive a free book and get updates when new Misty M. Beller books release, go to https://mistymbeller.com/freebook

ALSO BY MISTY M. BELLER

**Brothers of Sapphire Ranch**

Healing the Mountain Man's Heart

Marrying the Mountain Man's Best Friend

Protecting the Mountain Man's Treasure

Earning the Mountain Man's Trust

Winning the Mountain Man's Love

Pretending to be the Mountain Man's Wife

Guarding the Mountain Man's Secret

Saving the Mountain Man's Legacy

**Sisters of the Rockies**

Rocky Mountain Rendezvous

Rocky Mountain Promise

Rocky Mountain Journey

**The Mountain Series**

The Lady and the Mountain Man

The Lady and the Mountain Doctor

The Lady and the Mountain Fire

The Lady and the Mountain Promise

The Lady and the Mountain Call

This Treacherous Journey

This Wilderness Journey

This Freedom Journey (novella)

This Courageous Journey

This Homeward Journey

This Daring Journey

This Healing Journey

**Call of the Rockies**

Freedom in the Mountain Wind

Hope in the Mountain River

Light in the Mountain Sky

Courage in the Mountain Wilderness

Faith in the Mountain Valley

Honor in the Mountain Refuge

Peace in the Mountain Haven

Grace on the Mountain Trail

Calm in the Mountain Storm

Joy on the Mountain Peak

**Brides of Laurent**

A Warrior's Heart

A Healer's Promise

A Daughter's Courage

**Hearts of Montana**

Hope's Highest Mountain

Love's Mountain Quest

Faith's Mountain Home

Honor's Mountain Promise

**Texas Rancher Trilogy**

The Rancher Takes a Cook

The Ranger Takes a Bride

The Rancher Takes a Cowgirl

**Wyoming Mountain Tales**

A Pony Express Romance

A Rocky Mountain Romance

A Sweetwater River Romance

A Mountain Christmas Romance

# ABOUT THE AUTHOR

**Misty M. Beller** is an ECPA and *USA Today* bestselling author with over 1 million books sold. She writes romantic mountain stories, set on the 1800s frontier and woven with the truth of God's love.

Raised on a farm and surrounded by family, Misty developed her love for horses, history, and adventure. These days, her husband and children provide fresh adventure every day, keeping her both grounded and crazy.

Misty's passion is to create inspiring Christian fiction infused with the grandeur of the mountains, writing historical romance that displays God's abundant love through the twists and turns in the lives of her characters.

Sharing her stories with readers is a dream come true for Misty. She writes from her country home in South Carolina and escapes to the mountains any chance she gets.

**Connect with Misty at <u>www.MistyMBeller.com</u>**

www.ingramcontent.com/pod-product-compliance
Lightning Source LLC
Chambersburg PA
CBHW061240310726
48971CB00007B/2154